T0157696

"What happened to the shepherds after they viewed the birth of Jesus in Bethlehem? The Bible does not mention them again. Jan Hill has written a novel exploring the lives of everyday people in Christ's time on earth. Life under Roman domination weighed heavily on all Jews, but especially on the poor. The shepherds have vital lives of their own, but always intersecting with the life of Christ. Their joys and sorrows triumphs and tragedies, are like ours, down-to-earth, but always part of a higher purpose. In Shepherds Find Their Shepherd come explore the world of Joel, Jeshur, Nathan, their families, as well as the Wise Men, as they find meaning in the life of Christ.

William E. Ellis, author of "A Man of Books and a Man of the People": E. Y. Mullins and the "Crisis of Moderate Southern Baptist Leadership."

Shepherds Find Their Shepherd

JAN HILL

WESTBOW
PRESS®
A DIVISION OF THOMAS NELSON
& ZONDERVAN

Copyright © 2017 Jan Hill.

All rights reserved. No part of this book may be used or reproduced by any means, graphic, electronic, or mechanical, including photocopying, recording, taping or by any information storage retrieval system without the written permission of the author except in the case of brief quotations embodied in critical articles and reviews.

This is a work of fiction. All of the characters, names, incidents, places, organizations, and dialogue in this novel are either the products of the author's imagination or are used fictitiously.

WestBow Press books may be ordered through booksellers or by contacting:

WestBow Press
A Division of Thomas Nelson & Zondervan
1663 Liberty Drive
Bloomington, IN 47403
www.westbowpress.com
1 (866) 928-1240

Because of the dynamic nature of the Internet, any web addresses or links contained in this book may have changed since publication and may no longer be valid. The views expressed in this work are solely those of the author and do not necessarily reflect the views of the publisher, and the publisher hereby disclaims any responsibility for them.

Any people depicted in stock imagery provided by Thinkstock are models, and such images are being used for illustrative purposes only. Certain stock imagery © Thinkstock.

Scriptures taken from the Holy Bible, New International Version®, NIV®. Copyright © 1973, 1978, 1984, 2011 by Biblica, Inc.™ Used by permission of Zondervan. All rights reserved worldwide. www.zondervan.com The "NIV" and "New International Version" are trademarks registered in the United States Patent and Trademark Office by Biblica, Inc.™

ISBN: 978-1-5127-9945-3 (sc)
ISBN: 978-1-5127-9944-6 (hc)
ISBN: 978-1-5127-9946-0 (e)

Library of Congress Control Number: 2017912260

Print information available on the last page.

WestBow Press rev. date: 8/15/2017

Dedicated to my three grandchildren,
Nat, Michael, and Mallory.

Preface

I grew up in Ada, Oklahoma, where my life centered around going to school and church. My parents were Sunday school teachers. Daddy was a deacon, and Mother played the organ at the First Baptist Church. My brother, sister, and I were raised on the second row, organ side of the church.

Mother had the uncanny ability to discipline us with the eye in the back of her head. Our good upbringing did not only come from the exposure we received in Sunday school but from Mother's necessity to be at church every time the doors opened.

I remember our pastor, Dr. C. C. Morris, preached about sin and its effects. I remember the Sunday he said, "People don't tell others about Jesus anymore." My six-year-old heart moved me to promise God that I would always tell people about Jesus. I regret that many times since then, I have failed to keep that promise.

The story of how the shepherds "spread the word concerning what had been told them about this child and all who heard it" in Luke 2:17 has always gripped my heart. It brings my childhood promise to mind. Christmas cards and Christmas programs make me wonder about many behind-the-scenes activities that must have happened when Jesus was born. What did the angels look like? How long did the shepherds tell their story, and how did people react?

Christmas worship services and pageants we witnessed as missionaries in the Philippines gave me an Eastern cultural perspective of the story. A recent trip to Israel helped answer some of my many questions.

I look forward to the day when we know how it really happened.

Contents

Part 1

Part 2

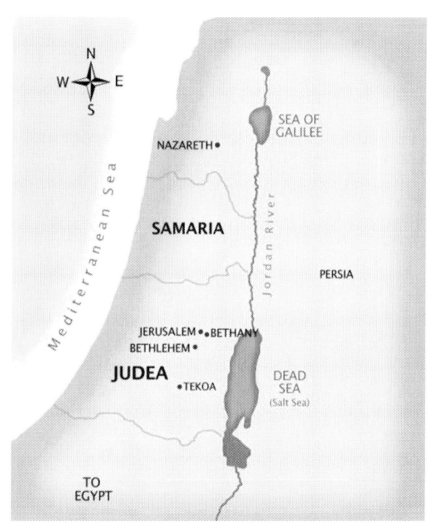

Map of Palestine

Part 1

Bethlehem

"Is that all the sheep, boys?"

"Yes, Father," Jeshur and Nathan replied as the lambs skittered up to avoid the dog's nip.

In the cool evening breeze, Joel stood at the opening of his pen. As he counted the flock passing single file between his legs, he examined them for wounds. "Twenty-five, twenty-six. Where is twenty-seven?"

At that moment, they heard the bleating of the youngest lamb and to their horror, saw a hyena dragging him off to his lair. The sheep in the pen set up a chorus of bleating, while their sheepdog fearlessly chased the hyena. The boys ran, screaming and throwing rocks at the four-legged thief. Joel aimed his slingshot, but the hyena was moving too fast. He followed the trickle of blood to the hyena's lair, howling at his adversary. Joel struck his heavy staff on stones. The boys continued their assault with a barrage of rocks until the hyena dropped its prey and stalked off. Joel gently carried the mangled lamb in his rough hands back to the campfire and poured oil on its wounds. The lamb gave a pitiful bleat and died.

Throughout Joel's twenty years of farming and raising sheep, he had always grieved over the loss of a lamb. He was a stern, pragmatic man, but underneath his hard exterior lay a soft heart. The village respected him for his honesty and reliability.

"You did all you could, Father. You are a good shepherd," commiserated the boys. The shepherds finished their simple meal in silence as they watched the cremation of their little lamb.

"That's the second lamb we've lost this spring," Joel grumbled. "We need to stay on our guard. Every lamb means food for our table." He began a story the boys had heard many times. "I am a poor shepherd who inherited five good acres of farmland from my father, who inherited it from his father. Your great-grandfather raised sheep and grew wheat and a few other crops on this same land. He planted all the olive and fig trees you see on the hillside yonder. Your grandfather built this sheep pen, and I remember carrying stones for its foundation. It had to be strong enough to withstand the occasional earthquakes we have."

In the distance, a wolf howled. Another answered his call. The boys huddled closer together.

"We lived out here in a tent my father built until we were able to build our little house in the village," Joel reminisced. He silently thanked God, who had given him four sons and one daughter. Jeshur, the eldest, was dependable, a deep thinker for his age, and never afraid to take responsibility. Nathan worshiped his big brother and was always full of questions. He had inherited a ten-stringed harp from a distant uncle and taught himself to play it while watching the sheep. He discovered that when the wind blew through the strings, it made an ethereal sound.

As darkness gathered, Joel continued. "My sons, you can be proud that you are of the tribe of Benjamin. We may be considered lowly shepherds from the smallest tribe of Israel. Even though we nearly died out many years ago, we are known for our skill in war and conquest. Our ancestors fought for the very ground you sit on."

"That's why you are so brave, Father. You know how to fight wild animals," said Nathan admiringly.

Joel paused and reflected on his family history. "You can be proud that your grandfather, Teman, was a shepherd," he continued. "Israel's greatest leaders were shepherds like Moses and King David. They learned how to be skilled leaders from raising sheep. You know how difficult sheep can be to lead."

The boys looked around, drinking in the peaceful scene that their ancestors had fought over. They could not imagine men killing each other over the land they had grown up on.

The sweet scent of new grass wafted on a gentle spring breeze. Sheepshearing was done, and most of the ewes had finished lambing. Joel's year-old lambs were ready to sell at the temple market in Jerusalem. "Just in time to be sacrificed for the Passover feasts," he commented. "We have to be careful that our lambs are perfect. If they have blemishes, the priests will reject them.

"The priests give us many rules to follow. Nevertheless, be glad you boys come from a line of good Jewish ancestors. Our Jewish heritage came through Abraham. Just as the dawn of a new day comes softly and gradually grows stronger, pushing back the dark, it became stronger little by little, like the brilliance of the noonday sun. King David was our fearless leader. We had the temple in Jerusalem, where our people worshiped. But now, like the pale evening light, our strength is weakening as Rome's might creeps over the land. We still have the temple, but the priests are cowardly because of Rome's control. People are losing their way and are confused in the darkness. We need a new day, a new light for the Jews."

"Why is the temple so important, Father?" asked Jeshur.

"It's God's home on earth," replied Joel. "In the beginning, the temple site was a rocky threshing floor on Mount Moriah. King David bought it from Ornan in Jerusalem. He built an altar there and offered sacrifices to God. His son, Solomon, built the first temple in the same place. My grandparents said it was magnificent in every way. Sadly, the Babylonians destroyed it.

"After many years of conflict and bloodshed, our intimidating, half-Jewish king, Herod, is now enlarging and beautifying the second temple. On our special feast days, Jews from many distant lands come together to worship God. But we are not as united as we once were. Many of our people have married foreigners and worship other gods." He sighed and shook his head.

Joel's story slipped into a lament. "We have very little to hope for with the Romans in power. We are like sheep among Roman wolves. They consider us part of their new colony. They are even taking a census of our people so they can tax us more. I fear our short time of peace will soon be lost, and then what will become of us? Our leaders are not strong enough to overthrow them. We need another King David to defeat them." He sighed again, feeling the weight of his children's future on his shoulders.

Joel lay down, becoming the "door" of the old sheep pen. Since it was spring, the sheep slept in the open. In cold weather, they stayed at the back of the pen under a roofed shelter. With the loss of a lamb and the scent of new lambs in the air, they were more cautious, watching for wolves and jackals. The boys rolled out their mats of woven straw and settled down as Joel took the first watch of the night.

Joel gazed at the luminous starry universe as it began to appear. He watched the stars' familiar path, taking note of the time according to their journey across the heavens. His eyes grew heavy with sleep.

Suddenly, an explosion of lightning split the air. The shepherds screamed in terror and then fell trembling to the ground. They saw an angel dressed in dazzling light, hovering in the air. The sheep jumped and bleated. The dog barked in a frenzy, and predators, following the scent of newborn lambs, turned tail and ran.

"Don't be afraid," said the angel calmly. "I am a messenger sent to you from almighty God." The barking and bleating suddenly hushed. "The peace you so earnestly wish for has come today," announced the angel. "Because God loves you, he has sent you and all the world his greatest gift, the Messiah. He is your Savior, Christ the Lord." The angel's words echoed throughout the hills like waves of the sea.

"He has just been born to a young couple, Joseph and Mary, in King David's town of Bethlehem. You will find him snuggly wrapped up and lying in a cow's manger."

"In a manger?" asked the trembling shepherds. "How can the Messiah be lying in a lowly cow's manger? Even our baby brother, Ezer, has a crib."

With a wave of his arm, the angel joined an angelic choir that filled the heavens, singing glorious music such as the shepherds had never heard. "Glory to God in the highest, and on earth, peace to men on whom God's favor rests." The music ricocheted in splendor, echoing throughout every hill and valley.

The shepherds were mesmerized at the sight and sounds. They were so filled with joy and wonder that even as old men, they talked about this moment. The Savior had come with the promise of peace to a troubled world. God had sent them His Son. They could hardly believe it. A gift from almighty God. Who would ever dream of being offered God's only Son as a blessing? All their troubles seemed to vanish as they thought of God's favor. When the angels finished their remarkable concert, they flew single file back to heaven, singing as they went, and finally dimming into a tiny speck of light.

"They left heaven's door opened a crack to remind us of their visit," mused Joel, pointing to the light. "I can still see it."

"I don't understand. Why did God want his Son to be born here in this little town?" asked Jeshur.

"This isn't just a small, sleepy town," Joel reminded his son. "This is where Ruth gleaned the fields of Boaz. Their son Obed raised his son, Jesse, who raised his son David. The prophet Samuel anointed David and later crowned him king right here in Bethlehem. That's why the angel called it 'David's city.' But you boys go and find the new Messiah while I guard the sheep."

A Star of Wonder

Across the eastern world, stargazers took note of a new star in the heavens. Many theorists began to speculate about its significance.

"Caspar, Balthazar, come out to the balcony and look. I see a new star, and it seems to be moving westward," mused Melchior, a renowned Zoroastrian priest.

The Persian scholar who studied the stars pointed. "It seems to be heading for Arabia or maybe Judea in the west. I wonder what it means."

The three men watched, mesmerized by the lustrous star slowly moving to the west. Melchior went inside, opened a dusty old trunk, and rummaged through his scrolls. "I wonder if these ancient scrolls might tell us something. The Jews left them behind in their haste to flee their Babylonian captivity," he explained.

"I remember my grandfather telling of a prophetic message he heard as a boy," mused Caspar. "It concerned a star in Judah promising a new ruler for the Jews."

"Why do you think this star could fit that prophecy? Sometimes an unusual combination of stars means some kind of disaster," countered Balthazar.

"Is it a combination of stars or just one large star?" asked Caspar, back out on the balcony for a second look. "Whatever it is, it must signify something very important."

Melchior unrolled the fragile scrolls carefully. By candlelight, the three men pored over the ancient writings into the night.

"Ah, here it is in the scroll of Numbers. 'A star will come out of Jacob. A scepter will rise out of Israel ...'" read Melchior.

"Israel!" the others exclaimed.

The three scholars met at Melchior's home in Susa every three years to pursue their favorite passion of looking for signs in the patterns and movement of the stars. They believed stars announced the births and deaths of kings. They discussed the implications of this truly magnificent star. They had never seen anything like it.

"I think we should follow the star and see if there is a new king in Israel," suggested Melchior. "We have historical records of their kings—King David and King Solomon, among others. I believe the star is announcing that a most divine king has been born, a new king for the Jews. Why don't we follow the star and see if it's true?"

"Go all the way to Israel? How long would that take?" asked Caspar, rubbing his hip. "Are we physically fit for such a journey? There are some high mountains, not to mention the Euphrates River and barren deserts. Such a journey will take more than a year," he estimated.

"Our camels can join the merchants who know the trade routes to Jerusalem," said Balthazar, always ready for adventure.

At midnight the men looked at the mysterious star again, moving slowly like a brilliant diamond in the sky, beckoning them to follow.

God's Gift in a Cave

The angels' announcement stirred wonder and curiosity in the shepherds' hearts. Jeshur and Nathan grabbed burning sticks from the fire for torches and set off for Bethlehem, wondering how they would ever find the newborn baby. They hurried down the familiar path in the dark valley across the stream and up the hill to the village, set on a ridge higher than the surrounding hills. They hurried down the one street that ran through town to a prominent alley close to the main gate. Every house was dark, and the market was closed. Near the city gate they saw lights and a group of people sitting in the courtyard of the old Bethlehem Inn. They made their way among the many groups of travelers sitting around in the courtyard who were spinning their tales to the others there to register for the census.

"Let's ask the innkeeper if he knows about a baby," suggested Jeshur.

The innkeeper, a tall, lean man, was very busy but stopped long enough to talk to the boys.

"Oh, yes," Isaac answered. "My wife, Abigail, is helping with the new baby now. They are down in the cave in back where we keep our animals."

"In a cave?" The boys looked at each other in disbelief. How could the Savior of the world be born in a cave? They made their way through the crowd, passing what they thought was an ordinary evening, not realizing that it was the most extraordinary evening ever known.

The young men entered the cave hesitantly. A woman greeted them. "How may I help you? I am Abigail, the innkeeper's wife."

In the torchlight, a young couple about their age sat on a pile of hay. The Christ child lay beside them in the cow's manger, just as the angel had described.

"God be with you." The boys bowed. "We are shepherds, Jeshur and

Nathan, sons of Joel. An angel told us the Messiah was born here tonight. Is it true?"

"An angel? My goodness. Yes," replied Abigail. "Come in."

The young man stood by his wife. "An angel told you about our baby? Yes. it's true. He's just been born. We're so happy. We've named him Jesus, as God instructed. I'm Joseph, and this is my wife, Mary. We laid Jesus here in the cow's manger."

The shepherds knelt beside the manger, their minds trying to understand why lowly shepherds were the first to see the King of Peace and why he was born in a lowly cave.

"He looks like our little brother, Ezer," Nathan whispered.

"Shh," Jeshur said, nudging him. "This is the baby the angel told us about. He's only a baby now, but someday everyone will know him as the King who brings peace to the whole world. Just think. Tonight we lost a lamb but received the gift of a king." They faintly heard the angels' music again. The boys looked around. The only sounds coming from the cave were the movement of a few sheep and cows nearby settling in for the night.

Abigail gave Mary something to eat and drink, then gathered up her things. "You need to rest, Mary. I'm sorry the inn is overflowing with travelers tonight, but I think you will be comfortable enough here. There's plenty of straw for your bed. I'll be leaving now, but my brother's house out toward Ramah will be vacant in two days. You can rent it if you wish. You are welcome to stay here until then."

"Thank you," said Joseph. "We are very grateful. I'll register for the census tomorrow. Mary and the baby will stay here." He turned to the shepherds. "You said an angel told you about us?"

"Yes, we were out on the hill with our sheep when we saw an angel in the sky. He told us that God was sending his anointed Messiah as a gift to the world and we would be greatly favored," answered Jeshur.

"And then the whole sky lit up with angels singing beautiful music like we had never heard before," said Nathan. "We came to see if the story was true."

Mary smiled as the boys told their amazing story. "I'm so honored that God chose me to be the mother of his Son. Wait and see. I know God will use him to change the world. He has already changed our lives. He has blessed us with such joy and peace—more than we've ever known." She caressed the baby's soft little cheek.

On the way back to their father, the boys told many people how they had seen angels and how Jesus, the promised Messiah, had just been born in the cave down behind the old Bethlehem Inn. Most could not believe their story. Some ridiculed them. They skipped along, their feet barely touching the ground, their incredible story becoming more real to them each time they told it. Joel was anxious to hear what they had learned.

"Oh, Father, we saw the baby the angel told us about."

Both boys talked at once they were so excited. "He was born in a cave behind the inn just like the angel said. He was all wrapped up and lying asleep in the cow's manger. We talked to Mary and Joseph. They said he would change the whole world."

"Wait a minute. I know we all saw the angel," agreed their father, "but how can a king be born in a cave? I can't believe someone born under those circumstances could be our king. It just isn't possible. It doesn't fit our teachings. Our rabbis tell us that the Messiah will come to us in power to bring us peace."

How could Jeshur and Nathan disagree with their father? Their sense of joy suddenly vanished. Yet they could hardly sleep that night.

The next morning, Jeshur faintly heard the angel's music once again as the brothers walked the familiar path home. It seemed to swirl about his head. He felt a sudden urge to sing, as the events of the previous evening crowded his mind. Surely their mother would believe their story.

Joel's simple two-room stone house was located at the end of a cluster of houses. The floor consisted of mud mixed and smoothed with lime. A flight of stairs on the outside of the back wall led to the roof, its beams covered with a woven straw mat and clay. Two narrow windows let in limited sunlight. His wife, Adah, was busy out in the courtyard milking the goats. His daughter, Tabitha, was playing with three-year old Onam and baby Ezer when the boys arrived.

Breathlessly the boys told their story.

"Last night we saw a shining angel up in the sky. He told us about a baby being born here in Bethlehem. The angel said the baby was the Messiah sent by God to the world. Then the whole sky filled with angels who sang so beautifully. They sounded like the wind plucking the strings of a thousand harps! We ran to the inn and found the baby and his parents down in the cave where they keep the animals, just like the angel told us. We found him all wrapped up and asleep in a cow's manger."

Shepherds' house

"Wait a minute! In a cow's manger?" Adah exclaimed.

"Yes, he looked a lot like baby Ezer," added Nathan, "only smaller."

Tabitha was fascinated. "Oh, I wish I could have seen him too," she cried.

"You can go to the cave and see them today. Joseph and Mary are here because of the census, and tomorrow they will move into Abigail's brother's house out toward Ramah," said Jeshur. "We heard them talking about it."

"We'll take them some goat milk and cheese," said Adah, wiping her hands as she finished her milking chores. "I just don't know how this can be the Messiah we've hoped and prayed for all these years. But whoever they are, the young couple needs our help. We may be poor shepherds, but we have a house where all of you children were born. Your father made our crib so each of you had a decent bed. But why would the Messiah be born in a cave and have just a cow's manger for a bed? Why would God treat the Messiah like that? Besides, didn't your aunt Maacah swear she met a stranger on his way to Jerusalem last year who claimed to be the Messiah? How do we know who to believe?"

The morning sun spread across the land, waking the countryside with its resplendent beams. But it fell far short of the entrance of the cave where Joseph and Mary slept with their newborn baby. Joseph left the cave quietly, letting Mary and the baby sleep. He made his way to the inn and stood in line to see the innkeeper, busily attending to his guests. Joseph noticed a little red-headed boy playing tag with other children. *Someday Jesus will be running around like that,* he thought, smiling.

"Good morning, sir. I'm Joseph from Nazareth. Thank you for letting my wife and me stay in your cave last night. After our long trip, we needed to find a room where she could rest and have her baby. Your wife was a big help too. She said we could rent her brother's house tomorrow. I hope you don't mind if we stay in the cave again tonight."

Isaac, a red-bearded man with a permanent frown, managed a smile.

"My wife says you have a fine baby boy. Sorry he had to be born in the cave, but as you can see, we have every room occupied. We'll be glad for you to stay tonight, free of charge." The little red-headed boy came running to him.

"This is my little boy, Lud." Isaac picked him up and hugged him. "Sorry for the interruption. I'm so busy here I don't see much of him. So you came all the way from Nazareth?"

"Yes, I need to know how to get to the Roman garrison," Joseph replied.

Isaac launched into a diatribe on the evils of Roman authority.

"The inn is full of people who have traveled from all over the country to pay their taxes," he said. "The Romans come in, take over our land and then charge us for their being here. The taxes are too high, and they set all kinds of rules and regulations. We hear rumors of their cruel penalties, even crucifixions for minor offenses. The Roman garrison is down the street there. Just follow all those people headed in the same direction. It's run by a couple of Roman families who have lived here for years. Most people turn their backs or hide when they see them coming."

A Star's Significance

The three Zoroastrian priests talked until dawn about the significance of the new star.

"An old Persian legend tells of a rising star predicting the birth of a ruler. It goes on to say he is a divine figure in fire and light," recounted Melchior pacing back and forth. "If this coincides with the prophecy we found in the Hebrew scriptures, it is a truly historical occasion we don't want to miss. There are merchant roads that lead to Jerusalem. It is a strategic city, one that a ruler of this stature could come from. It would be to our advantage to welcome him and show him honor from our country." Caspar and Balthazar agreed.

"Father, did you see the new star in the sky?" Churan, Melchior's eldest son, burst into the room. He was a handsome youth with twinkling eyes. Being an impetuous young man, he often spoke before he thought. Seeing his father's visitors, he bowed. "Excuse me, I hope I didn't interrupt your conversation. I saw the star on my way home from my friend's wedding feast and knew you would be interested."

"Yes, son, we were just discussing its significance and thinking of following it."

"You're going to chase a star? What a great adventure. May I join you?"

The older men looked askance at each other. The thought of taking a rash young man on a long journey startled them.

Melchior took a deep breath. "Son, I need you to take care of things here while I'm gone." Churan was disappointed but knew it was pointless to argue with his father. The men set about plotting their course, listing supplies and gifts for a new king of such stature.

Mary's Story

Joel and Adah could talk of nothing but the angels' visit.

"Jeshur, you and Nathan saw the baby just as the angel described, so you are totally convinced that you have seen the son of God. It is easy for you to believe because you saw him," said Joel, rubbing his neck. "But what if you're wrong? What if it's a hoax?"

"Papa, when you see him, you will know he is God's Son," they earnestly assured him.

As the news spread, their story drew a curious crowd outside their gate. Jeshur and Nathan excitedly told their story over and over. Some of their friends taunted them.

"Who sees angels?" one of them asked. "Someone who is fixing to die," scoffed another. The crowd began to laugh as they left.

"Let them laugh," said Jeshur. "Someday they will believe me."

Meanwhile Adah milked the goats and prepared cheese and bread for the new family and their son, whoever he was. Tabitha was so excited she twirled around the room. She couldn't wait to meet this family the angels had talked about.

Adah and Tabitha walked down the town's one main road to the inn.

"Mother, do you believe this is God's son like the angel told Papa and the boys?"

"Maybe we will find out when we visit them," answered Adah. "I think if he is God's son, God will let us know."

They made their way down to the cave behind the inn carrying the goat's milk, cheese, and bread.

"God be with you," Adah called as she entered the cave. "I am Adah, and this is my daughter, Tabitha."

"Oh, do come in," Mary greeted them.

Adah continued, "I'm the mother of Jeshur and Nathan, Joel's sons who visited you last night. They told us about you and your baby. I thought you might need some food."

Tabitha tiptoed over to look at the sleeping baby in the manger while the women talked. She smiled and hummed a little tune she often hummed when she took care of her baby brother, Ezer.

"Thank you," said Mary. "You are so kind. We came from Nazareth, and we don't know anyone here. My husband, Joseph, is at the Roman garrison registering us for the census since his father was originally from here."

"Nazareth? You've come a long way. How hard the trip must have been for you. Is this your first baby?" inquired Adah. She bent over the manger to see the baby, who was beginning to stir.

"Oh yes, he is a special child." Mary picked him up and cradled him in her arms. "About a year ago, when Joseph and I pledged to be married, I had a visit from an angel telling me I was to be the mother of God's Son, the Messiah. At first I was astounded. Then I remembered my mother telling me how every Jewish girl hopes she will be the mother of the Messiah. When my mother realized that she wasn't chosen, she often prayed that I would be the one. I asked the angel how this could happen since I was a virgin. The angel explained, 'Nothing is impossible with God.' I felt honored to be chosen and accepted this news even though I didn't understand everything.

"The angel went on to say that my barren cousin, Elizabeth, the wife of an elderly rabbi, was going to have a child in her old age. Now that was hard to believe. My mother and I decided to visit her in Judea since we hadn't seen her for a long time. Sure enough, she was six months pregnant. Not only that, she told me her baby leaped in her womb the moment she saw me. She began to prophesy that I was pregnant and she was honored that the mother of her Lord would come for a visit.

"She told us how her husband, Zechariah, who had been chosen to serve in the temple in Jerusalem, saw the angel Gabriel while he was ministering in the holy of holies. The angel told him he would have a son who would become a famous preacher and would announce the coming of the Messiah. He was to name him John. Zechariah was so surprised that his barren wife would become pregnant that he couldn't believe the angel. As a result, the angel struck him dumb. Elizabeth told me 'You can see for yourself. He has lost his voice. He can't say a word.'

"It was true," Mary continued. "We stayed about three months, and we never heard him speak. Even so, we had a wonderful visit. Elizabeth's faith encouraged me and prepared me for what lay ahead. My faith in God grew stronger. I was ready to be his servant.

"When I came home obviously pregnant and told Joseph about the angel's message, he didn't believe me. I thought he was going to break our engagement. But an angel came to him in a dream and told him to fulfill our wedding vows. You see, this child's real father is Almighty God. I can't understand everything, but I have faith that God asked me to raise his Son. I'm happy that he chose me to bring Jesus into the world." Then she looked at the baby adoringly.

"But here, in Bethlehem, in a cave?" asked Adah, looking around in astonishment.

"I know it's hard to understand, but we are happy to part of God's plan," responded Mary. The baby began to cry, so she patted his head and rocked him. "We will move tomorrow to Abigail's brother's house near Ramah."

"Yes, I know the place. May we come to visit you there?" asked Adah.

"Of course," said Mary. "You are always welcome."

With that Adah and Tabitha left the young mother and her newborn baby. Adah shook her head, wondering how God's miraculous plan could be so inconvenient.

On their way home, Tabitha skipped along. "Mother, what do you think of Mary's story? Don't you think she was telling the truth? And Jesus is so beautiful. He opened his eyes for a moment. He has such sparkling eyes. I'm so happy I got to see him."

"And no one could ever dream up a story like Mary's," Adah said, sighing. "God surely does great and wonderful things, but in such strange ways. Having his Son born in a cave? I just can't understand it all. Let's tell your father Mary's story and see if he believes it."

Joel listened somewhat impatiently to Adah's account of the visit to Mary. "What do you make of it?" she asked.

Joel hedged. "The moon is nearly full," he said gruffly. "I have things to do, and it's time to get the sheep to the temple." He walked around the room.

"The priests always say they prefer our sheep from Bethlehem because they are perfect. I'll think about it on the way."

"But Joel ..." Adah cried as he left the room.

Joel took Jeshur and Nathan to help him herd a choice flock of sheep destined to be sacrificed for the sins of the people. Travelers would come from near and far, some from as far away as Antioch, Rome, and Alexandria, where they worshiped in synagogues. They believed that God lived in the holy of holies in the temple in Jerusalem and wanted to worship him there.

Herding jostling sheep from Bethlehem to Jerusalem slowed the shepherds' journey, but their sheepdog helped keep the sheep together. Along the crowded road, Jeshur and Nathan excitedly shared their story about seeing angels and the new Messiah. They told everyone how the angel explained that a virgin gave birth to the Messiah in a cave in Bethlehem. They even invited them to go and see him there.

That evening Joel and the boys herded the sheep into a temporary fold built of thorn bushes outside the walls of Jerusalem. Joel built a fire, and other shepherds joined them, adding their sheep to the fold.

The shepherds sat around the fire visiting and telling stories. The amazing story of the angels told by Joel and his sons provoked a variety of responses, from outright disbelief to joy and wonder. Men shook their heads and stroked their beards. What could the angels' visit mean? How could one man bring peace to Israel and the whole world?

"Is the boys' story true, Joel?" asked a shepherd from the Elah Valley.

"Yes, I know it is hard to believe, but I saw the angels too," Joel admitted.

The story spread from one to another, even those in other groups. Many people questioned the boys. The next morning, each shepherd called his own sheep out of the fold.

Later, by the time Joel and his sons got to the temple courts, their story had arrived ahead of them. The shepherds had to tell their story again and again. The more Jeshur and Nathan told the story, the more convinced they were in their own hearts that the Baby Jesus was the Son of God.

Magi Came from the East

The three Persian scholars sent servants scurrying here and there to procure the needed stock of food and straw for their camels. Each camel and mule had to carry enough supplies to cross the Syrian desert, to Aleppo, Damascus, and farther.

Melchior sent his steward to the market to find a caravan headed for Jerusalem. People crowded around hawkers as they advertised their wares. Elbowing his way through the melee, the steward approached a caravan leader.

"Excuse me sir, where is your caravan going?" asked the steward.

"We're headed east to Mesopotamia, Syria, and Judea, then down to Egypt," the leader said.

"When do you leave?" the steward asked.

"As soon as we sell our goods and get fresh supplies," the leader replied. "We have a long journey ahead so we have to take plenty of food and water. We'll leave tomorrow at sunset." He patted the neck of his camel as he spoke.

"Would you permit three men to join your caravan as far as Jerusalem? They have their own camels and mules," assured the steward.

"Well, I don't know," replied the leader. "Do they know what a rough trip it is? And can they keep up the pace?"

"I'm sure they can," assured the steward. "They are experienced travelers."

"What is their business? Why do they want to go to Jerusalem?" asked the leader.

"They are scholars, sir. They study the meaning of the stars. See that star overhead? It's so bright you can see it even in daylight. They want to follow it to Jerusalem."

The leader shaded his eyes and squinted at the star's remarkable glinting radiance. "How do they know it's headed for Jerusalem?" he asked.

"I don't know," answered the steward, scratching his head. "I just know they think the star will lead them to a new king. I assure you they won't be of any trouble to your caravan."

"Humph!" replied the leader. "If they can keep up with us, that's all we ask. Tell them to bring their own supplies and be here at sunset tomorrow." He turned and left.

When the steward returned to Melchior, his news caused a flurry of last-minute packing. Servants ran here and there fulfilling the scholars' demands. The men's thrill of adventure overcame the tension and possible dangers of the long trip. They made a pact to stay together, whatever happened.

"I feel the star will lead us to great blessing," Caspar said. "The trip will be worth all our trouble."

"This is the trip of a lifetime," exulted Balthazar.

Melchior agreed. "Tomorrow! I can hardly wait."

At sunset the next day, a hundred camels loaded with silks and spices lined up, nose to tail. Hardened camel drivers laughed and laid bets as to how long the three refined scholars would last.

The caravan traveled by night to avoid the heat of day. A donkey whose master either rode or walked alongside led the caravan, setting the pace as they journeyed through the desert. The tinkling bells of the camels made a reassuring sound that all was well.

The three scholars had aged somewhat since their last trip and had also become more accustomed to soft-pillowed chairs. They had forgotten how inconveniently stiff camel seats were. But they soon remembered how to sway from side to side in rhythm with the camels.

The caravan passed over ancient battlegrounds, drenched with the blood and tears of warriors and martyrs. Following the star, a gem of hope, made the scholars anxious to meet that ultimate Peacemaker. They hoped in their hearts that he would end all violence and suffering. As they traveled, they wondered how this new King in Judea would answer all the perplexing problems of law and justice, resulting in peace to all generations. They skirted other lands where war was the schedule of the day—where battles had been lost and won and lost and won again. When would it all end?

What did war accomplish? Was it worth the bloodshed and pain? The loss of fathers and sons? What did it gain? An extra inch of soil renamed, reclaimed?

A crowd gathered wherever the merchant caravan stopped for supplies along its journey. Children begged for treats or coins. Hawkers displayed their wares. As they bought and sold, they asked, "Where are you going? What news do you have?"

The three scholars responded, "We are going to see the newborn king of the Jews in Judea. We are following the star that announced his birth."

"We were disturbed when we saw that star," some said. "We thought it meant famine or war."

"We believe we'll find the Messiah who will bring peace and goodwill to everyone," replied the scholars.

A Blessed Visit

"Mother, may we go and visit Joseph and Mary and the baby again?" Tabitha begged a few days later. "I'm sure they have moved by now." The family could talk of nothing else.

Joel made a blanket of soft sheepskin, and Adah wove a fine wool blanket for Baby Jesus. They didn't have much themselves, but they wanted to help the young family.

Adah took all of the children, including Baby Ezer, carrying him in her robe, to visit Mary and Joseph while Joel stayed with his sheep. Joseph greeted them at the gate and led them into the small, two-room house. In the back room was an earthen oven where they cooked. Stairs led to an elevated platform where they slept above the stove.

Mary let Adah hold Jesus, who gazed up at her and grasped her finger. "Behold, the gift of God," Adah murmured. "What sparkling eyes," she added. The boys crowded around, wishing Jesus were older so they could all go out and play.

"He looks like a real baby," whispered four-year-old Onam. The mothers enjoyed talking about their babies while the boys played in the courtyard.

"We just returned from taking Jesus to the synagogue for his circumcision," Mary told her new friends. "He was a good baby throughout the ceremony and didn't cry much. The rabbi permitted Joseph to perform the circumcision, which made it more meaningful for us. We named him Jesus, following the instructions the angel gave us. The angel said that he would also be called Prince of Peace, Almighty God, Wonderful Counselor. We will take him to the temple soon for his dedication."

"After you go to Jerusalem, will you come back here or go home?" Jeshur asked Joseph.

"As the Lord wishes, we will stay here until Mary and the baby are strong enough to make the trip back to Nazareth," Joseph replied. "I must get back to my carpenter shop. I lose business every day I stay away." He didn't like the fact that rumors were already spreading about how the authorities might react to a new king being born in Bethlehem.

Joseph and Mary traveled with their new baby through the throngs of humanity on their way to Jerusalem. They felt the thrill of fulfilling the Jewish law to dedicate God's Son at the temple. The wall of the city came into view. Towers glinted in the sun-washed sky. They made their way through the sheep gate, where Joseph bought a pair of doves for Mary's cleansing and sin offering. At the temple, several young couples came with their babies for their consecration to God. After the priest's blessing, Mary and Joseph turned to leave when an elderly man pushed his way through the crowd.

"Excuse me, I'm Simeon. The Holy Spirit led me to you. I've just heard the most exciting story from some shepherds, and I must see this baby," he explained to Mary and Joseph. "I have been promised by God that I would see the Messiah with my own eyes before I die. May I …?" He took Jesus in his arms and gazed at him. He lifted Jesus up and prayed, "Thank you, Lord, for letting me see your only Son, your gift to the world. He will bring us peace and be a light and revelation to the Gentiles."

Joseph and Mary were amazed at Simeon's words. He blessed them as he handed Jesus back to his mother.

"This child is destined to cause the falling and rising of many in Israel and will be a sign that will be spoken against, so that the thoughts of many hearts will be revealed. Mary, a sword will pierce your own soul."

Mary looked at Joseph and shuddered. "What did Simeon mean?" they wondered.

Simeon raised his hands, looked up, and smiled. "Now I can die in peace, for God has fulfilled his promise to me." Then he turned to Joseph and Mary. "I almost forgot. There is someone from the tribe of Asher who wants to meet you. She's been waiting to see the Messiah for seventy-seven years. She spends her time here at the temple worshiping God day and night."

A diminutive, wrinkled, gray-haired Anna hobbled up at that moment.

With outstretched arms, she exclaimed in her feeble voice, "God be praised." She cradled Jesus in her bony arms.

"He has answered my prayers. I have been waiting to see this child, God's own Son, all these years." With her face wreathed in smiles, she continued. "He will bring us peace and redeem us of all our sins. God be with you."

Joseph and Mary, a little overwhelmed by all the comments, examined Jesus to see if there were some outward indication that he was the Messiah. All they saw was a baby with sparkling eyes. They fulfilled their religious requirements and returned to the little house in Bethlehem.

"I wish we could go back to Nazareth and show Jesus to our families," sighed Mary, regretfully.

"You are not strong enough yet to make the long trip, and besides, it would be hard to take the baby that far. We must wait in Bethlehem until God tells us it is safe to travel. Remember, this is God's child, not ours," Joseph added.

Joel and his family continued to visit Joseph and Mary and Jesus from time to time, becoming fast friends.

A New King for the Jews?

The wise men sighed wearily as they made their way to the inn of a friend in Damascus. Their year's journey was beginning to wear on them.

"Where are you going this time?" asked Frya. His servant wiped the men's feet with wet towels, and another served them a cool drink.

"We are following the star of the new king of the Jews born in Judea," the travelers answered.

"New king? They need a new king!" he said disgustedly. "I was in Judea last year on business. King Herod is a madman. He doesn't trust anyone and even killed two of his five sons he was so suspicious of them. He has so many wives I wonder which one finally bore a son. The last two royal children were daughters born several years ago.

"They need a new king, but he will have a hard time taking Herod's throne. How can this new king conquer Rome's power? The Jews have no real freedom. Rome controls all of Judea. I saw spies everywhere. Herod taxes people every year when in the past they only paid once in a lifetime. He has to tax them to pay for all of his building projects, especially his monstrous palace."

The three scholars discussed possibilities of how to approach King Herod. They counted their liabilities as they set out, knowing they followed a divine star and its creator.

The Sabbath

Tabitha played with Ezer out in the courtyard while her mother tended the goats and their small vegetable patch. Ezer seemed such a happy baby, cooing and talking in his own private language. His fair skin and jet-black hair set him apart from his siblings, tanned by the desert sun. Ezer's big black eyes rimmed with curly lashes followed Tabitha's every move. His brothers made little toys for him out of clay and teased him and carried him on their backs. But Tabitha was his favorite. She was learning how to comb, spin, and weave the wool from her father's sheep. As she wove, she sang a little song. Ezer always laughed and clapped his hands when she sang.

"You are getting to be a big boy, Ezer," cried his mother when he took his first steps. "You are already a year old, and look how big you are." Ezer balanced himself carefully, then fell clinging to his mother's robe. "Before long we won't be able to keep up with you." She picked him up and hugged him. Ezer, eager to try more steps, squirmed out of her arms.

"When we celebrate your second birthday, we will have a weaning feast for you, Ezer," she promised.

While the older boys were busy helping their father with the sheep, Ezer played with four-year-old Onam. Onam always entertained Ezer with his little games of hide-and-seek among the clay jars and stacks of bedrolls. When Joel came home, tired from working in the fields, Ezer greeted him with hugs and kisses. His childish laughter seemed to erase the trials of the day.

The family followed the teachings of the Torah, handed down from their forefathers. The parents taught their children as much as they understood about God. A mezuzah on their doorpost contained scriptures to remind them of the Torah. They kissed it every time they entered or left the house.

The family members were careful not to touch blood or any dead creature according to the law. Adah carefully drained blood from the animals they cooked and ate. She made unleavened matzah and lit candles for the observance of the sabbath every Friday at sundown. At the end of the Passover meal, it was the custom for the youngest child to ask, "Why is this night different from all other nights?" Joel would answer by telling the ancient story of their deliverance from bondage in Egypt, many years ago. He then repeated the blessing: "Blessed art Thou, O Eternal! Who redeems Israel. Blessed art Thou, O Eternal. Our God! King of the universe, Creator of the fruit of the vine."

The life of a shepherd was hard, but Joel enjoyed being up on the hill with the sheep. Since the angels' visit Joel thought more about God and the gift of his son, Jesus, and how they had actually seen him. Jeshur and Nathan had just arrived with food and water. Their conversation turned often to the angels' visit.

"They were right up there." Joel pointed to eastern sky so familiar to him. "They left a new star in the sky. It's still there. In fact, it is brighter and seems to be getting nearer," Joel observed.

What Child Is This?

The merchant caravan forded the river near Jericho. By sunrise Jerusalem appeared on the horizon. The caravan leader bid farewell to his three extra travelers. They had stayed the course. All bets were off.

"You'll find the palace up in the northwest section, beyond the market." the leader added. "God be with you."

The weary magi had traveled all night. But at the sight of the gleaming bastions of the great walled city they experienced a joy both mysterious and profound. After a lifetime of study and nearly two years of travel, the scholars were about to experience the fulfillment of their dream for hope and peace. Since they were headed to the palace, their eyes followed the ghettos of the city, not the star.

"I see an inn where we can sleep and refresh ourselves for a few hours," Melchior said. "I know we're close to our destination, but I need to rest and prepare for our visit." Caspar and Balthazar readily agreed.

By afternoon the magi set off for the palace. This was unlike any palace they had ever seen. Huge blocks of glistening white marble greeted their eyes. Three highly decorated towers stood in the background.

The scholars' imposing array assured them of immediate entry at the Damascus Gate. The guard promptly ushered the imposing nobility into the palace grounds. They passed fountains, hanging gardens, canals, several groves of trees with long pathways meandering through them, gold and silver vases, and statues beyond description. The sun beaming through skylights danced on floors of polished marble.

At the outer court, a procurator greeted them.

"What is your business with the king?" he asked.

"We have come from Persia to see King Herod and the new king," announced Melchior.

"New king?" The procurator disappeared through a side curtain to consult his assistants. After a short time, he reappeared and bowed.

"Your excellencies, the king will see you in his chamber."

He led them past a lavish display of sculpture and art objects into the inner court to the king's throne room illuminated by five great chandeliers. The three scholars bowed to the ground.

King Herod, a short, obese man, dressed in a heavily ornamented robe, sat on a gilded throne. Two large, half-naked, muscular servants fanned him continually with ostrich plumes. At the snap of a finger, servants came with trays laden with grapes and figs.

Melchior addressed King Herod. "Your royal highness, it is with great pleasure that we who study the stars have come from Persia to greet you and to wish you good health and God's peace. We also extend our congratulations to you and your family and especially to the new king who has been born to you. We have read the prophecy in the ancient scriptures of his birth in Judea and followed his star for nearly two years. It has led us to this very city. Now we return to you the ancient scrolls left by the Jews during their Babylonian captivity as a gift to be restored to your people."

Herod listened carefully and then leaned forward, saying, "We are happy to receive you, and thank you for returning our ancient scriptures. I don't know your source of information, but we do not have a new king here. I am king, and we do not need a new one." He frowned. His rising anger was obvious to all.

The scholars felt uneasy. Something didn't feel right. Had they made the long trip for nothing? Had the star led them astray?

"We have heard many rumors that some shepherds out on the hills somewhere saw angels and a baby king born in a cave," continued King Herod with a contemptuous curl of his lip. "All of Jerusalem is in an uproar over the news. We have received many reports of a messiah appearing now and then, but these men turn out to be imposters. Everyone knows that when the Messiah comes, he will be fully grown. He will come on a cloud, attended by angels. He will come to the temple, the earthly home of his Father. However, since you have come so far, I will consult my wives to see if there is a new child born among them. My chief priests and scholars

28

will search these scriptures you have brought to see if there is indeed any prophecy of a new king. Until then my chief minister will give you a tour of the palace."

And what a tour it was. Herod's reputation as a builder showed that he had spared nothing to make this the grandest palace in the world. They passed by several large banquet halls, one filled with guests celebrating an elaborate feast with dancing and music.

After the tour, the minister led the scholars back to the throne room. King Herod, surrounded by his chief priests, exclaimed, "We are still examining the scrolls you brought us. We would be remiss if we did not invite you to dine with us this evening and spend the night, since you have had such a long journey."

The scholars were happy to accept the king's invitation, even though it meant waiting a little longer to accomplish their goal of finding the new king. In a lavish dining area, they reclined on luxurious couches, where they dined on roasted lamb and veal. Wine flowed freely, and musicians played stringed instruments, which enhanced the occasion.

Later Herod and the chief priests joined them. "We have good news for you," the king announced. "We've found that there is indeed a new king prophesied in the scriptures, and he will come from Bethlehem."

One of the chief priests opened the scroll and read from the book of Micah: "But you, Bethlehem Ephratha, though you are small among the clans of Judah, out of you will come for me one who will be ruler over Israel." The scholars glanced at each other in surprise.

King Herod nodded. "We have also recently seen the star but did not attach any great significance to it. Now tell me, when did you first see it?"

"Let's see. I don't have my records with me, but I saw it several moons ago," hedged Balthazar. "Caspar, when did you first see it?" Caspar and Melchior shook their heads.

"It could have been there long before we saw it following a different path," explained Melchior.

"I see," mused the king. "Then you must go and visit the new king since you have traveled so far. Bethlehem is a small town, so you shouldn't have much trouble finding him. And since we now know the story is true, please return and let me know where he is, so that I can also pay tribute to Israel's new majesty. I wish you well." A servant led them to a beautiful bedroom. On their couches lay three silk robes decorated with the king's special insignia.

Early the next morning, Melchior woke the others. "My sleep was troubled last night. I had the strangest dream. An angel warned me not to come back to see King Herod after we find the new king but to go home by a different route."

"That's strange. I had the same dream," said Caspar.

"So did I," said Balthazar, yawning and stretching. "It must have been God's angel sending us a message."

"Let's leave as soon as possible. We don't want the king to know any more than what we've already told him," said Melchior. "He knows we followed the star for nearly two years. I regret that we were not more cautious with our information."

The scholars left as dawn broke over the eastern sky. The brilliant star they had followed so earnestly, beckoned them once more. Bethlehem was only six miles away, and the men felt they could easily get there by midday. They mounted their camels and headed south with mixed feelings.

"Why didn't we find that second prophecy about the Messiah's birthplace ourselves?" chided Caspar. "We should have spent more time searching the scriptures."

"I agree," said Melchior. "We wouldn't have alerted Herod about the child. I think we should follow the angel's advice and go home through Egypt."

The others agreed even though it would be a longer trip. "I feel it's best for all concerned," Melchior added.

"Look at the star. It's turning south!" exclaimed Balthazar. The men looked up to see the most amazing move of the star.

"I've never seen a star move south," exclaimed Caspar. The others agreed it was most unusual but rejoiced that God was leading them to the promised Messiah. By midmorning the gleaming star hung motionless in the sky.

Praying for divine direction, the three made their way to the Bethlehem inn. Abigail, the innkeeper's wife, heard their story and said, "Yes, I'm the midwife who delivered the baby. He lives with his parents, Joseph and Mary, in my brother's house out toward Ramah. They named him Jesus."

The three scholars were ecstatic. They made their way down a narrow road toward Ramah. A toddler played out in the courtyard of a small house. The star shone overhead.

"Jesus, come inside. It's time to eat," called his mother.

Melchior stopped and dismounted from his camel.

"Is your name Jesus?" he asked as he knelt before a child with sparkling eyes. Melchior's voice was almost shaking. Mary came out as the other men quickly dismounted their camels.

"Joseph," she called. "We have visitors." Joseph came out and joined his stunned wife as they took in the sight of the imposing guests kneeling before Jesus. They bowed in that awesome moment, amazed to be in the very presence of the new king.

"Here is my gift of myrrh for the king of kings," said Balthazar. Melchior presented him frankincense, while Caspar gave him gold.

Melchior turned to Joseph and Mary. "God be with you. We come in peace. We are priests and scholars from the east who study the stars. We knew this one," he gestured upward, "was of the greatest significance and have followed it here."

Joseph and Mary looked up at the radiant star in surprise.

Melchior's voice failed, he was so overcome with joy and emotion. "We have followed this star for two years, believing it would lead us to the new king. We have come to worship and honor him."

Joseph and Mary were overwhelmed with the rich gifts.

"Almighty God has sent you here," said Joseph. "We are honored that you would come from so far away."

They served their visitors a refreshing drink as they all shared details of their experiences of the past two years and marveled at how wonderfully God had brought them together.

"We do not want to cause alarm, but we inquired of King Herod where we would find the new king," said Melchior. "He seemed agitated over the scriptures that prophesied a new king would be born right here in Bethlehem. I hope you will take every precaution."

"God has given us great responsibility in raising his Son," Joseph said. "I'm sure he will protect us." Mary nodded in agreement.

"We were also warned by an angel in a dream last night not to report back to King Herod that we have found the new king," said Caspar. "The angel instructed us to go home by a different route. We have decided to travel through Egypt. It is a longer route, but we want to follow the angel's instructions. We'll get supplies, spend the night at the inn, and be off tomorrow," Balthazar added.

"We must bid you farewell, Joseph and Mary," said Melchior, "but our hearts are overjoyed. We will share your story wherever we go." The men left, rejoicing and thanking God that their two-year-long mission had been accomplished. They had found the king. It was time for a good night's rest. It was time to go home.

In the middle of the night, the scholars were wakened by a knock on their door.

"Who could it be at this hour?" Melchior groggily asked, groping for his robe.

"I hope it's not Roman soldiers," said Caspar, anxiously.

Balthazar took the oil lamp, crept to the door, and asked, "Who's there?"

"It's me, Joseph. I need to speak to you. It is urgent."

Balthazar quickly opened the door, and Joseph rushed in.

"I'm so sorry to wake you like this," said Joseph, "but an angel warned me in a dream tonight that we must leave Bethlehem as soon as possible and go to Egypt, where we have friends. We hurriedly packed our things, but the innkeeper just informed us there is no caravan until tomorrow night. Could we possibly travel with you?"

Melchior turned to his friends. "Would you like to take Joseph and Mary and the new king to Egypt?"

"Of course," they agreed.

"We must hurry. The Romans may have already set up a road block," said Joseph.

The imposing family, dressed in their royal robes traveling by camel and mule, raised no suspicions as they arrived at a road block.

Roman soldiers bowed and called out, "Make way for the king."

Melchior chuckled and murmured to the others, "Truer words were never spoken."

Regally robed Joseph and Mary, carrying a toddler swathed in another of Herod's robes, were filled with gratitude for God's provision. Their royal robes guaranteed them safe passage all the way to Egypt. The scholars also marveled that they had a part in the escape of the new king.

While Joseph and Mary were sad to leave their homeland, they knew it was necessary to protect the child.

After bidding the little family good-bye in Egypt, the scholars set their course for home. They had no star to follow, but God's love overflowed in their hearts.

"We'll never see Jerusalem again," Melchior said, sighing, "but we saw something even greater—the new king. We were never more at home than when we were with him."

The three scholars shared their miraculous experience with fellow travelers along the way, and a new thread of joy began to glow in Persia.

Three wise men

Rumors

Adah and Tabitha, carrying a basket of goat cheese, looked forward to their trips to the market. Mother and daughter had a close relationship, especially since Tabitha was their only daughter. They picked their way along the familiar, dusty road to the crowded market. Near the city gate they saw a camel caravan unloading bags of grain, silks, and spices.

Trips to the market were also a challenge. Joel's family was known as the "shepherds who saw angels." Beggars, children, and hawkers called out, "Here comes the angel family," as Adah and Tabitha walked by. They hurried on, trying to ignore them.

The market was the source of news about who was getting married, the next new baby, whose elderly parent had died. Adah hoped to barter her goat cheese for the bread the city was famous for. Tabitha looked forward to seeing some of her friends. They passed by blankets and stalls of grain, utensils, leather goods, tools, lamps, dyes, herbs, fruit, and vegetables. They avoided beggars' outstretched hands and a leper's call, "unclean, unclean." They headed to the bakery and cheese stalls, where customers bargained for the best price.

"You should see my Ezer," Adah bragged as she met the town gossip, Hodesh. "He's growing so fast, and now he's walking and running all over the place. He just turned two, and we had a weaning celebration for him. He is truly a gift from God."

"My two-year-old is cranky. She's teething," said Hodesh, lifting her crying toddler from her hip to show Adah. "It's just that painful season for her." She rocked her back and forth, trying to quiet her. She drew nearer and lowered her voice.

"Did you hear about the Roman soldiers who were here?" She always seemed to be the source of the latest news. Adah checked to see if there were any soldiers nearby, shifted her basket, and leaned forward in eagerness.

"It seems they were looking for someone, but I didn't hear who." Hodesh glanced over her shoulder. "I think it might have had something to do with those three strangers with loaded camels decorated like you would not believe. They came all the way from Persia. My cousin told me she watered their camels. She said they were very rich, dressed in silk robes and turbans. They spent the night at the inn. The innkeeper said they had been traveling for nearly two years."

Hodesh went on her way, sharing her gossip with any who would listen.

"What brought them all the way to Bethlehem?" Adah wondered. "Did it have something to do with the new king?

Adah dismissed the thought in her hurry to get to the cheese stall. Customers were already waiting.

Adah easily sold her cheese, then stopped at the bakery to buy bread. No one could avoid the smell of freshly baked bread. She glanced up at the sky and realized the cool of the morning had melted into the heat of the day.

"Hurry, Tabitha, we must get home," Adah whispered. "The sun is already high, and Nathan will wonder why we're late." They overheard a group of men talking as they passed by.

"Say, did you see that bright star in the sky last night? It's so bright you could see it early this morning, and it's right over Bethlehem. I wonder what kind of sign it is."

"I hope it doesn't mean drought or trouble of some kind," another replied.

Adah and Tabitha passed a trio of soldiers who paid them no attention as they hurried home, relieved to see that Nathan had taken good care of Onam and Ezer.

Out in the field Joel watched his son, Jeshur, skillfully lead the sheep to a new patch of weeds. Joel thanked God for all his children, who seemed to grow up as quickly as the weeds on the hillside and bloom like wildflowers. They stopped for a brief lunch of barley bread and figs when Joel heard his dog bark. He turned to see Nathan running up the hill, crying, his face ashen.

"Father, come quickly," he gasped. "The Roman soldiers came to our house and killed Ezer. They nearly killed Onam too, but Mother stopped them. There was so much blood! They've killed a lot of babies in the village."

Joel stiffened. In utter shock, he forced himself to move as if in slow motion to cope with reality. He put Jeshur in charge of the sheep and ran home with Nathan. On the way, they met people running, screaming, beating their breasts, and tearing their robes.

Adah sat in their courtyard rocking her lifeless baby Ezer. She was speechless.

"Father, the Roman soldiers came. There was nothing we could do," cried Tabitha, still trembling.

"How? Why?" Joel's mind spun, trying to take this in. "What has happened to my family and this whole village?" He could hear the cries of women wailing in the distance. Adah was past screaming. She was in total shock.

Joel cringed in horror at the sight of his precious son in Adah's arms. Those beautiful black eyes with curly lashes closed forever. The family tore their robes and wailed in despair. Their innocent child, the one who brought such delight, was gone. Why should his family be victims of such unthinkable violence? Why did callous Roman soldiers ravage the peaceful town of Bethlehem? Why kill little children? They sat in utter silence, their thoughts swirling.

Adah came to the sobering reality that they needed to bury their precious baby. She washed the little body, recalling how Ezer used to squirm and laugh when she bathed him. She rubbed her lifeless cherub with oil, then took linen strips and bound his body as she had done at the death of her elderly parents.

Mourners up and down the streets blended their voices in a cacophony of agony. They blessed those who grieved, chanting, "May you be comforted among all the mourners of Zion and Jerusalem." "Why kill innocent children?" they asked each other. Bethlehem had never experienced grief of such epic proportions. Because of their common tribal bond, the community decided to have one burial ceremony. They chose to mark the common gravesite with a stone; each of the nineteen babies' names was carved on it. Rabbi Caleb led the mourners in the funeral service even though his own son was among the dead.

Afterward, during a mourning feast of bread and wine, the men huddled together in small groups. They nursed the fear of who would be next. "Why were little children killed and not others?"

"And in broad daylight. Some nerve."

"I just heard the innkeeper was murdered, and his wife and child are missing."

"How did the soldiers know which families had small children?"

Rumors raced from house to house, and fear gripped every heart.

"Why can't the Romans leave us alone? They're monsters," the men grumbled.

"I didn't see Joseph and Mary at the burial ceremony," whispered Tabitha to her brothers as they left the funeral. "I wonder what happened to them."

"Let's go see," suggested Jeshur. They found the familiar little house on the opposite edge of town completely empty.

"They must have heard something and escaped," said Tabitha. "But where did they go? I wonder if they knew something was going to happen."

Adah slipped home reluctantly after the ceremony, instinctively knowing she must cleanse her house of the ghastly sight of murder before her family arrived. She shuddered as she reached the familiar gate and touched the mezuzah. Was God there? If so, why hadn't he protected her baby? She paused at the entry, dreading to go in. The place the family called home looked so different now, as if haunted by the specter of death.

Her tears mingled with Ezer's blood, her little lamb, as she knelt and mopped the stone floor. Memories of the small and mindless things of Ezer's life were now a treasure. Adah gathered the little toys Ezer's brothers had made for him—toys that had once filled little Ezer's heart with giggles of delight. She set them on a shelf to provoke future memories of a day she wished had never happened. She washed his tiny garments and spread them on a bush to dry. Would she ever need them again?

"Maybe some for grandchildren," she mused with a sigh.

Trips to the market, meeting others who had lost their little ones, brought tears of agony to the women of Bethlehem, all dressed in sackcloth. Ten of the women who had lost babies decided to meet for a few days at the now-empty house of Joseph and Mary to share their heartaches.

The older women greeted the younger, so new in parenthood and still fresh in their grief. Each bonded with the others in their sorrow. They felt a mixture of compassion and revulsion.

Rhoda shared how her child on that fateful day had just learned to say her name. "That soldier's face will haunt me forever," she cried.

Sarah grimaced. "My child had just taken his first steps." Several nodded and commented that their babies, too, had just started walking.

"I was nursing my Abidan when the soldier came bursting in," cried Ruth. "What could I do?" She wiped imaginary blood from her breast and arms. "What would my son have become if he had been permitted to grow up?"

"I didn't mind carrying mine on my back while I worked out in the field," added Martha. "He was such a happy baby."

"This was my first child," cried a young mother, wiping her eyes. "He looked just like his father," she sobbed. "I want to hold him just one more time. My soul is empty because my arms are empty. I will never hold another child as beautiful as he."

"I suffered a miscarriage because I fought to protect my baby," said Ephrath. "I lost two children that day. What is womanhood about, anyway?"

The women's shared agony gave way to quiet sobbing. No one wanted to move or sleep or eat. Each sat in silence, trying to comprehend the events of that terrible day.

In the gathering darkness, Adah slipped out the gate for a breath of air. She wiped her eyes and looked up at the star that her family had watched from night to night. It had shone brightly over Joseph and Mary's house, but now it was faded into the shape of a cross, the sign of criminal punishment. She shuddered and turned to go inside. There she saw a cross marked on the gate post. "What does all this mean?" she wondered. "Bethlehem, the city of bread, has become the city of the dead."

The women's anger flooded over their grief the next day.

"I will never forget what it felt like to touch my cold, dead baby," moaned Judith. "What is more important than human life? What law did our babies break to pay with their very lives? If only my husband had been home, he would have protected us."

"No," Babatha responded. "The soldiers would have killed him too."

"Were our little ones a threat to the Roman government?" asked Chloe, the rabbi's wife. "We have three daughters but lost our only son. If he'd had the chance to live to manhood, he would have been Bethlehem's next rabbi." She wept on Judith's shoulder.

"Will the soldiers come again and kill our other children?" Miriam wondered. "Why our children? Is God punishing us for some reason?"

A contagious fear gripped every heart. Each mother looked helplessly to the others, all trying to make sense of the matter. Roman soldiers seemed to be everywhere, eyeing the people with suspicion.

"What happened to the family who lived here?" asked Judith. "I've heard so many rumors about them."

Adah shook her head and fell silent. She had also wondered what happened to the young couple and their toddler, Jesus. They seemed like such a nice family. At least Jesus was spared from the massacre. Was he actually going to be a king like the angel promised?

"We visited them several times," answered Adah. "They were such a wonderful young couple." She paused and then decided to share with her friends the story of the angel's visit. In her gentle voice, she described the announcement of the birth of the Messiah and the promise of peace and good will to all people. She had seen the promised Messiah herself in that very house. It seemed to help ease the women's pain and suffering. But where was he now?

Because they had handled the bodies of their dead children, the mothers were required to take a purification bath on the third and seventh days to fulfill the Jewish law. As nerves became more settled and normal feelings began to return, they decided to take a walk.

"Let's go to Rachel's tomb," suggested Adah. "I went there once with my family. We could walk to the tomb and back in a day." They sent word inviting the other grieving mothers to join them.

The next day as the mothers were reunited, a wail rose from among them. They beat their breasts, overwhelmed once again with their loss. Greetings and hugs from kindred souls lifted their spirits as they shared their experiences.

The women's visit to her tomb helped them remember that Rachel, too, suffered the loss of her son Joseph, more than a century ago. When her husband, Jacob, moved his family from Padan Aram to Canaan, Rachel went into labor near Bethlehem. She died giving birth to her son, Benjamin.

Jacob paid great tribute to his wife by building a tomb of eleven rocks representing the tribes of Israel.

Benjamin, Jacob's twelfth son, followed his father as a tribal leader. Some of his descendants were King Saul, Judge Ehud, and the prophet Jeremiah.

The women took note that God had cared for all of their forefathers and brought them to this good land. They left Rachel's tomb reassured that even in perilous times, God would protect them as he had in the past. The women bade each other goodbye, determined to bring renewed hope to their families.

Adah was devastated over losing a child, but spending time with the other mothers eased her sorrow. She returned home to find a despondent atmosphere. Tabitha and Nathan had done their best to manage without her and cope with Onam's outbursts of anger and tears. Joel and Jeshur had stayed in the fields to watch the sheep and avoid the situation entirely.

Now a mantle of silence mixed with anxiety seemed to hover in the air. Fear lurked in every shadow of the night. Every time a soldier rode by or someone stopped at the gate, their hearts skipped a beat. Adah resolved to be strong by recalling the promise of the angel who said Jesus would bring peace on earth and good will for all people. She wanted peace in her own heart and peace for her family.

When the children quarreled, Adah realized she had to be strong and calm them down. She sang songs and told them stories of their forefathers. Still, the horror of the event came back to haunt her dreams. When she tried to express her thoughts to Joel, he seemed at a loss for words. He never spoke of his lost son. His pain was too deep to express. He often sat, staring into nothingness, numb with grief. Jeshur and Nathan stayed with their father out on the hills with the sheep as much as possible. The pastoral scene comforted them all in their distress.

Tabitha hung her head and sobbed while spinning. She could not sing as she remembered how much Ezer enjoyed her songs.

Onam especially didn't understand. His four-year-old incurable curiosity kept him searching for his brother through the house. He kept looking for Ezer among the jars of oil and cushions as if they were still playing hide-and-seek. He just knew that he would spy him peeking around the corner, laughing.

"Papa, where is Ezer?" cried Onam, climbing into his father's lap.

Joel shook his head, noncommittal, stone faced.

"He is in heaven with God," Adah gently replied, picking him up.

"Well, when is he coming back?"

She set him down and hugged him. "He's not coming back, Onam. God took him to his new home in heaven."

"I don't like God." said Onam.

"You mustn't say that, Onam. God is love, and he loves you even though we cannot understand his ways."

This conversation was repeated many times until Onam finally realized that Ezer was gone from his life forever. He often cried himself to sleep.

Part 2

A New Day

The smells of spring wafted on the cool morning air. The lambing had increased Joel's flock, and his sons helped with the sheep shearing, always a family event. Joel admired his sons, Nathan and Onam, dressed in short sleeveless under-tunics revealing their youth and vigor as they climbed the hill. They observed the purple-tinted mountain chain of Moab and Gilead in the distance. Joel breathed deeply of the fresh spring air and looked with pride at his son Jeshur tending his sheep on the next hill.

Joel whistled a familiar greeting. Jeshur responded, happy to be tending his own flock. Jeshur had a wife from among his own tribe, thanks to his father. Joel felt that Hannah was a good choice for him and with her Jeshur would continue the family line. Joel looked forward to becoming a grandfather soon. He silently thanked God for his blessing.

Nathan led the sheep to new patches of grass while Joel cut a sturdy limb from an old oak tree. He whittled it into a staff for Onam, now a teenager and old enough to be in charge of the sheep. The staff was tall for him, but Onam would soon grow taller.

"You will need this to help you climb those rugged mountains when grass is scarce in the valleys," explained Joel. "Remember to keep it with you always in case you meet a jackal or wolf. I use mine when I'm rescuing lambs too."

Joel patiently taught his teenage son the dangers he would face in shepherding sheep. Joel also fashioned a rod from a short, thick branch and attached nails on one end for Onam's protection.

Joel seemed pleased with his work and extended the staff and rod, but Onam's heart sank as he took them from his father. Onam's mind was filled with memories of his first trip to Jerusalem for the Passover celebration.

He vividly remembered the sights of the outside world as throngs of people came from distant lands. He often daydreamed of how to escape the boring job of raising sheep on a lonely hill. He wanted to see what the world had to offer.

"Are you listening, Onam?" Joel brought him back to reality, patiently telling him about the way to herd sheep, where to find grass and water, and when to move on.

"Yes, Papa." Onam bowed his head, glumly accepting the task.

Joel, softening his voice, concluded, "I must go back to the farm now, but Nathan will help you."

Onam sat on an old stump and gazed at the quiet pastoral scene. "Look at my father and my brothers," he complained to Nathan. "You all enjoy the simple life of watching sheep out on the hills and playing your harp. Surely there is more to life than raising sheep and farming."

"But that's our life," replied Nathan. "That's all our family has ever done. Jeshur and I took our turn shepherding. Now you are the shepherd. In our tradition, the youngest son becomes the family's shepherd."

So Onam reluctantly shepherded his father's sheep, all the while dreaming of ways to escape such a dull life.

Joel farmed the plot of land back of their house. He managed to grow enough crops for his family and hay to feed the sheep during winter. As age encroached upon him, he rarely ventured out to the hills, and he increasingly relied on Onam.

Tabitha

Grinding wheat to flour was a daily ritual for Tabitha and her mother. They push-pulled the old millstone back and forth in their courtyard. The rhythmic sounds echoed in the ears of the two women

Adah sighed. *What will I do without Tabitha?* Long ago she had been promised to Joel's distant kinsman's son, and now the time of their betrothal was approaching. *He will be a fortunate husband, and her dowry will be most helpful. Tabitha learns quickly and is so helpful. Besides, she is a beautiful girl, and others have asked for her.*

Tabitha was troubled when her father told her of her betrothal arrangements. She had met him only once at a family festival. She tried to recall his appearance but realized it was hopeless.

"My kinsmen will be coming soon," Joel said. "We must prepare for their visit."

On the appointed day, Samuel, a sheep herder, and his son, Ira, visited Joel's family. Ira and his brother raised their father's sheep south of Bethlehem on the Judean ridge near Tekoa. Samuel, quite a jolly man, was short in comparison to his lanky son. He always spoke in a lusty voice for both of them. Introverted Ira seemed nervous and hardly looked at Tabitha when they were introduced.

"He's a fine young man, a hard worker, dependable and honest. He will be a good husband," Samuel assured Joel.

Tabitha hung her head while the two fathers talked about their children's future. "I've had your son picked out for my daughter for years," Joel replied. "I'm sure they will be a good match."

Joel's family and some of their neighbors and Rabbi Caleb gathered around to serve as witnesses as soft-spoken Ira gave Tabitha a gold ring pledging their marriage.

"See by this ring you are set apart for me, according to the law of Moses and of Israel," he quoted in a shaky voice. In a year, they would marry.

Adah tried to comfort her daughter, who broke into tears after the men left. "Don't worry about getting married. Ira comes from a good family of shepherds like ours. You will learn to love your husband like you love your brothers."

With the help of relatives and friends, Joel's family scrimped and saved for a year to give their only daughter a fine wedding ceremony. Tabitha eventually resigned herself to the fact that she had no choice but to marry.

Ira and his family arrived on their wedding day for Tabitha, perfumed and ornately dressed. She joined her new husband, wearing a crown and heavy veil. Ira was also splendidly dressed. After a wedding feast, the relatives blessed them as the newlyweds left her parents' home. The whole town witnessed the torchlight procession down Bethlehem's one main road ending at the groom's parents' home in a neighboring community. Feasting and celebration continued for another six days.

Ira and Tabitha traveled slowly up the inclines of rugged hills and down the ravines, leading their small herd of goats, wedding gifts from their parents, to the high plateau of Tekoa. Tabitha carried candles and a mezuzah, a gift from her mother, who also reminded her of the importance of observing the sabbath. On their way, Ira talked about Tekoa as if it were a paradise. They arrived near sundown high on a barren ridge south of Bethlehem.

"We're here," announced Ira.

"But where shall we live?" asked Tabitha, looking around.

"This tent is our home. You will live with me here," Ira explained. "Here comes my brother, Daniel."

"I'm glad you arrived before dark," said Daniel. "My wife and I live down the hill a bit. She's glad to have another woman up here. She has food prepared for us."

Daniel's wife, Debra, greeted them warmly, and Tabitha was relieved to have another woman living nearby. After a simple meal, the new couple wearily climbed back up the hill, with Tabitha wondering about her prospects of living in a goatskin tent.

"See this pile of rocks," exclaimed Ira. "I have been collecting rocks for the past year so one day we can build our own house." Tabitha smiled and silently welcomed the promise of a future house.

Afternoon breezes kept the simmering summer heat under control. Tabitha could see distant mountain ranges on clear days and gradually adjusted to living "on top of the world." She also became accustomed to living alone in Ira's barren Judean "paradise" since he was often away moving the sheep to find grass.

Tabitha quickly became acquainted with the small group of shepherds' wives who lived farther down the ridge. She enjoyed exchanging stories with the women on their daily trips to the well. Each time Tabitha passed the rock pile she dreamed of her own house. She even collected a few rocks to add to the pile. She made up songs about the rock pile and her future house and sang softly to herself. But her heart yearned for something deeper, something she couldn't explain.

She often wondered, *Is this all there is to life?* The rock pile grew slowly.

Then one day, Ira suggested, "Let's mark the foundation for our house," Tabitha giggled with delight as they laid out small rocks designating the foundation. Her hopes and dreams for a house were now becoming a reality.

And sometime later, Tabitha found she was pregnant.

"You are going to be a father," she told Ira excitedly when he came back from a long week with the sheep. Then her eyes filled with tears.

"But I'm afraid I might have the baby while you are away." Ira was elated by her news but sad that she was so distressed. "I'll send word to your mother to care for you," Ira promised. Then he massaged her feet with oil until she relaxed and fell asleep.

Seven moons later, Adah and Nathan made their way over the rugged landscape to Tekoa. Tabitha waved excitedly from the tent as they trudged up the last steep ridge. Nathan wondered how Ira could raise sheep in such a barren wilderness. Adah wondered how her daughter could live in such a desolate place.

Adah hugged Tabitha and put her hand on her daughter's belly. "I didn't think I would live long enough to see your children," she said, laughing. Together they made preparations for the new child while Nathan helped Ira find new pasture for the sheep.

"Tabitha, I've watched babies being born, but I've never delivered one," commented Adah. "Is there a midwife nearby?"

"Yes, Mother, I have spoken to one of the shepherds' wives who's had experience as a midwife. She's willing to come and help," replied Tabitha.

A few weeks later, Miriam, the midwife, came to visit Tabitha to get acquainted. She explained to Tabitha and Adah how she would use birthing stones for the delivery.

Tabitha's water broke the following day. Adah ran quickly to Daniel and Debra's tent to send word to Ira and the midwife.

But Ira and Nathan were moving the sheep down the ridge to better feeding ground. So Debra sent word to the midwife then ran to help Tabitha.

By the time the midwife, Miriam, arrived, Tabitha was in full labor. When Miriam turned the baby, Tabitha's screams echoed up and down the ridge.

After two days, Tabitha and Miriam managed to deliver a healthy baby girl.

The new mother, filled with awe at the sight of her baby girl, said, "You look like your father. As soon as he arrives home, we will name you."

Tabitha was weak from her difficult delivery, but the midwife gave her herbs from her pouches, and Adah fed her *leben* she made from goat's milk. Tabitha slowly gained her strength with Adah's good care but wondered where Ira was. She felt she could not rest until she had shown him their baby.

Nathan arrived two days later, alone. In a sad voice, he told them that Ira was dead. "Ira saw his prize ram caught in a bush on the edge of a cliff while we were moving the sheep down the ridge," Nathan explained. "The ram suddenly bolted, knocking him over the cliff when he attempted to save it. I scrambled down the rocky slope as fast as I could, but Ira was gone. Daniel and I buried him at the bottom of the cliff under a pile of rocks."

Adah comforted Tabitha and encouraged her to return to their home, where she would be welcome. Tabitha left the goat-skin tent and rock pile, her dreams dashed like a pile of rocks. She felt strange returning home, a widow with a newly born baby.

Joel and the boys welcomed Tabitha and the new baby back home. Jeshur and his family came to greet her and see the new baby.

Joel cradled the baby in his arms, smiles crinkling his weathered face.

"God is gracious, and even in your loss, he has blessed our family with the gift of a new baby. It's been a long time since we've had a little one in the house," he said, chuckling. "She's a beautiful addition to our clan. What is her name?"

"I was waiting for her father to name her," Tabitha explained hesitantly. "Would you name her, Papa?"

Joel thought a moment. "We had chosen the name Elizabeth in case Onam was a girl, so her name is Elizabeth."

Onam

Onam dutifully took the sheep to pasture each morning and returned them to the pen in the evening, exhausted. He quickly learned how stubborn sheep could be. At first those dirty, smelly sheep didn't obey him because they didn't recognize his voice. When he guided them to a new feeding ground near someone's farm, those capricious creatures would head for the farm while Onam tried to call them back. Sometimes the farmers yelled at him when his sheep helped themselves to their crops.

One day Onam, tired from chasing a stray sheep, sat down under the shade of a tree to catch his breath. He looked up to see his flock scattering up the hill. He had to chase them through brush, scratching his bare, skinny legs.

Onam was constantly on his guard for jackals who appeared out of nowhere. Sometimes robbers stole stray sheep. Such a life fraught with danger, wore him out.

Onam dreamed of leaving home to find adventure and excitement elsewhere. He daydreamed of being rich like the wealthy merchants he once saw as a boy. The merchants, dressed in rich clothing and turbans, shouted at their servants to make way for them through the crowded market. Onam grumbled that he was the son of a poor shepherd, out in the field alone while his brothers were the ones who went to market. He also missed their family trips to Jerusalem for the Passover feast.

Onam was also puzzled about his father's practice of selling his sheep in Jerusalem.

"Father," Onam asked one day, "why do you take our very best sheep to sell at the temple market? Wouldn't they bring a very good price here in Bethlehem?"

"I know it would be easier to sell the sheep here, but it's an honor to sell them at the temple," his father responded. "The temple priests favor Bethlehem sheep because they are free of blemishes. People buy them to be sacrificed for their sins. The priest inspects each sheep for any blemishes. It has to be perfect in every way. Its blood is shed for the forgiveness of sin."

When Onam thought about his sheep being slain, he shivered, remembering how his little brother, Ezer, was slaughtered before his very eyes, much like a sacrificial lamb.

A year later, Joel finally permitted Onam to go to the temple market with his brothers. They taught him the required rituals to follow at the temple.

Jeshur introduced him to Reuben, their sheep buyer. "Oh, another shepherd who saw the angels," commented Reuben, smiling.

"No, I didn't see any," admitted Onam, feeling flustered that his family was always identified with the dubious honor of the angels' visit.

Eventually, Joel felt that Onam was trustworthy enough to take the sheep to the temple market by himself. The fact that his father trusted him with such an important responsibility welled up his confidence. Besides, it gave him a chance to get away from the boring life of shepherding. He knew the route well, and the sheep now knew his voice. He guided the lambs through the sheep gate at the temple, bathed each one, bathed himself in the temple pool, and took them to Reuben at the sheep market. He learned to haggle and congratulated himself for getting the best price of the day.

On his way home, the shekels jingled in his leather pouch. He fingered the coins, counting them again and again, wishing he could keep some for himself. But his father always knew how much he would receive. Besides, Joel trusted Onam and always gave him a percentage of the profit. He carefully saved his money for his future escape.

One day, after a profitable trip to the temple, Onam took a rocky path away from the rough, dusty road into a grove of trees. It was the dry season in Judea. Seeking relief from the heat, he pulled off his cloak with its colorful family design, slung it over his shoulder, and drank deeply from his wine skin. He nibbled a few bites of barley bread and watched as people walked to and fro. Each hurried after urgent unattended business. *Like ants*, he thought, *busily going here and there.*

A thin, ragged, red-bearded man impulsively joined him. He was breathing hard, as if he had been running. He coughed, bowed slightly, and asked, "Where are you going?"

"Bethlehem," responded Onam with a nod toward his destination. "Where are you going?"

"If God wills, I am also going that way." He glanced furtively around him. "What is your name?"

"Onam from the tribe of Benjamin. What is your name, and where are you from?"

"My name is Lud, and I am also from Bethlehem, but I live in Jerusalem."

Onam offered Lud the rest of his barley bread, which he ate greedily. They joined the stream of travelers on the road as they talked.

Lud continued, "My family lived in Bethlehem for many years. My father was the innkeeper there, and my mother the village midwife," he explained. "You may know that my father was murdered in cold blood by Roman soldiers. They were looking for a certain baby. Can you imagine, needing to find a baby they believed might be a king? And when my father tried to protect my mother and me, they killed him. They threatened to kill me and forced my mother to mark the houses where she had delivered babies two years old and under. The soldiers had orders from King Herod to find the baby and kill him. To make sure, they killed all the two-year-old males."

"Yes, Roman soldiers killed my baby brother, and they nearly killed me too," retorted Onam. "We always wondered why they killed the little ones. Why would God permit such things if he is a God of love?"

"Strange way to show love!" Lud agreed. "My father was always so busy with the inn he never had time to think about God. We never observed the Jewish laws. I can't understand why people worship at the temple. I watch them come and go, but they don't seem to act any differently from others."

"My family always observes the Jewish rituals, but they don't make much sense to me," Onam remarked. "One time my father and brothers were out on the hills with their sheep when they say they saw an angel come from heaven telling them a baby king had been born in Bethlehem. The angel said he was the Messiah. My brothers even found the baby and his parents in the cave behind the inn. Our family visited them when they moved to a house and we played with him, but he looked like any other baby. They all disappeared when the Roman soldiers killed the children. We've never heard anything more since then. Why would a king be born in a cave anyway? I think it was just nonsense. And all that killing for nothing."

Lud paused, shook his head, and said, "That's the baby the Roman soldiers were looking for. I remember seeing his mother with him in the cave when I helped feed the animals in there. My mother told me he was supposed to be a new king, but I didn't believe her story either. I think they were just an ordinary couple." He stopped and looked over his shoulder anxiously.

"Well," Lud continued, "the Roman soldiers let Mother and me go after they killed my father. We fled that same day to Jerusalem. Life has been very hard for us since then. I hate to see how hard my mother works. We barely have enough to eat. The only work I could find was in the market helping the vendors … that is until now."

Lud looked around again. "I promised myself if I ever had the chance I would kill the soldier who killed my father," he muttered. "One day my mother spotted him in the market and pointed him out to me. Today while I was helping myself to a few grains of wheat, he saw me and chased me." Lud's voice was shaking. "When he shouted and grabbed me, I managed to get the dagger out of his scabbard and stab him. I think I killed him. Soldiers saw us, but I outran them in the maze of the market. Some of the vendors accidentally blocked their path, and I got away." He stopped, opened his cloak, and disclosed the bloody dagger.

Onam gasped. "You must leave this country or the Romans will hunt you down and kill you."

"As the old saying goes, 'When an ant is pinched, does it not fight back and bite the hand of the man who struck it?'" quoted Lud. "Will you hide me until they quit looking for me?"

"We are poor shepherds, but you can help me with the sheep until it is safe for you to leave," offered Onam. "My father is old, and my brothers and I take care of our flock. We raise a few goats too. All very boring. I wish I could leave this kind of life."

"I know a man who would give us a good price for your sheep, no questions asked," responded Lud. "Just think, we could run away to Egypt, enjoy life. I know how to get what I want," he added. "People are so gullible; they are just tools in my hands." His laugh was cut short by the sound of approaching horses.

"Quick, I see soldiers coming," gasped Lud. He grabbed Onam's cloak and flung it on. Onam suddenly realized he had just become an accomplice to a murderer. He had become his own enemy. Lud humped over, walking lamely, leaning on Onam's staff like an old man as the soldiers rode by.

Onam took Lud back to their sheep pen, where he slept in the shelter at the back by day and roamed the countryside by night. Onam brought him food he stole from his home. They waited there until they were sure the Roman soldiers had given up searching for Lud.

One moonless night, the sheep blindly followed Onam's familiar voice out of the sheep pen to be sold for a tidy sum. When the deal was finished, Onam took the money and blindly followed Lud into the darkness to freedom from the dull life of shepherding.

Onam's theft left his father Joel enraged. He knew Onam was a troubled son, angry, impatient, and rebellious. But he thought Onam would eventually mature just as Jeshur and Nathan had. He paced back and forth, saying, "I trusted all my sons equally in good faith. Why has Onam betrayed me?"

Nathan remembered Onam telling him that he didn't like shepherding. He had even said he would leave if he had the chance. But they were all surprised that Onam would steal his own father's sheep. Joel had taught his children the proverb, "Stop listening to instruction and you will stray from words of knowledge."

The family drew together to help each other. Jeshur gave his father a pair of sheep from his own flock. At least they still had the goats and the small garden back of their house. Adah sold goat cheese in the market. Tabitha spun wool thread to sell to weavers. Later, as Joel's flocks slowly grew, they collected tallow from raw sheep fat to make soap to sell, thus adding to their income.

Nathan cared for his brother's flocks while Jeshur periodically searched the hills and valleys for Onam and the sheep. He called out to every flock he saw, hoping they would recognize his familiar voice, but to no avail.

Lud and Onam herded the sheep to Lud's friend, who paid a good price for them. They joined a caravan headed to Egypt, where they enjoyed "the good life," which came to an end all too soon.

They resorted to preying on travelers, robbing them of their mules and camels. Lud's buyers paid low prices for stolen goods. They lived among a Canaanite clan in Egypt, where Onam became fascinated with Joanna, a professional weaver. He began stealing sheep, shearing them, and supplying her with their wool to weave. Then they feasted on the sheep and sold their skin in the market. Joanna excelled in weaving robes with colorful designs that brought good prices.

During a drought in Egypt, shepherds drifted to the hills of Judea for better pastures. Onam convinced Lud to go back to Judea, where sheep were easier to steal. He also had a nagging desire to return home to see his family but kept it to himself. They took Joanna, who was pregnant by this time, with them. When they reached Bethlehem, Onam looked at his father's empty sheep pen across the hill. He felt shame and guilt as he thought of how Lud had convinced him to steal his father's flock. Lud recognized his distress and convinced him that they had a better life now.

"Remember, you were bored to tears when you were at home. Look how exciting your life is now," Lud remonstrated.

"I would like to see my family just once more," confessed Onam. "It's the Sabbath. Everyone will be at home."

In the dusky twilight, Onam crept up behind his boyhood home at the end of the neighborhood, his heart pounding wildly. He managed to get beyond the pitifully few sheep and goats corralled at the back and sneaked up the worn, familiar steps to the roof. He glimpsed his family in faint candlelight in the courtyard below. With bowed heads, they repeated the familiar sabbath blessing he had repeated since childhood. His emotions suddenly overwhelmed him when he saw how elderly his parents looked. Nathan had grown taller, and his little sister was now a beautiful lady. Elizabeth was now a little girl.

Jeshur has his own family now. So many changes.

He heard them murmuring but could not distinguish their words. His conscience stung him with accusations when he noticed his empty place at the table. Remorse and guilt swept over him. For a moment, he wanted to call out, *I'm here. I've come home. But no, I can never come home. They would never forgive me. I can never forgive myself.*

He turned to make his retreat, but the stairs made an unnerving noise. He darted back to the roof, leaping from rooftop to rooftop, clattering down the steps of the last house in the neighborhood. Nathan leaped up the stairs and tried to follow the would-be intruder, but Onam had a head start and vanished into the darkness. Lud and Joanna met him back at the empty sheep pen.

"Whoever it was, he got away. I just got a glimpse of him," said Nathan, panting for breath. "I wonder what he was up to."

Neighbors gathered to investigate the disturbance.

"Probably just some prowler," growled his father.

Lud, Onam, and Joanna made their way through the night to the road where caravans passed from Egypt to Jerusalem. They looked for someone to rob soon, for they were out of money and food, except for some figs they plucked from trees along the way. At the top of a hill, around a curve in the road, they prepared to ambush the next caravan that came along. They waited confidently, knowing the well-practiced routine. Joanna watched from a rocky ledge up the hill. She signaled that someone was coming.

An elderly man riding a camel and accompanied by a guide on a mule appeared. As they came around the bend, Onam stepped out and grabbed the camel's reins. Lud grabbed the guide and demanded money. The elderly passenger threw them a small bag that turned out to be one shekel in a bag of gravel. While Lud threatened the old man, two Roman soldiers came around the bend. They overpowered Lud and Onam, bound their hands with cords, and marched them to the dungeon in Jerusalem. Joanna followed at a discreet distance.

Visitors

Not long after, Joel saw a group of people standing at their gate. "Adah, I don't recognize them, but they may have news of Onam."

Adah peered out. "I think that is my cousin, Mary, from Galilee," she said hesitantly. "We always called her 'Madi.' But, my, how she has aged. Hurry and open the gate. We mustn't keep them waiting."

"God be with you," she greeted them.

"Mary is not well and keeps asking for you. I am Mica, her guardian," the man explained. "Her parents are old and can't travel, so they asked me to bring her to you, hoping that you can take care of her," he added. Adah quickly assured him she would be welcomed.

Madi seemed like a stranger to Adah even though they had grown up together. Adah hadn't seen her cousin since she married and left Galilee many years ago. Madi, always so witty, beautiful, and charming, the center of attention, was now a deranged woman. Illness had taken its toll. Adah sighed as she took responsibility for her cousin, wondering how they would manage.

Adah and Joel's grief over Onam was now compounded by having to care for a mentally ill woman. Madi paced the courtyard at night, sometimes moaning and screaming. Adah tried to calm her, to no avail. She asked Nathan to play his harp for her when he came home occasionally from the field. His music calmed her, but he was seldom there. He left his harp with her, but she tired of playing it.

Adah observed that Madi was attracted to their sheepdog's new puppy. She cuddled it and rocked it, which seemed to give her some peace. During the day Madi kept the puppy for companionship, but at night she wailed and cried. Sleep was almost impossible. Joel built a shelter up on the roof and slept there with the boys or out on the hill with the sheep. Adah and Tabitha took turns trying to comfort Madi, who continually moaned and screamed and paced the floor.

A young woman appeared at Joel's gate after three exhausting weeks.

"Is this the house of Joel and Adah?" she asked.

"Yes," Adah replied cautiously.

"I am Joanna, from Canaan. I am Onam's wife, and he asked me to bring you a letter."

Adah was speechless as she opened the gate.

The letter informed them that Onam was in jail, that Joanna was his wife and she was in "the family way." He begged forgiveness and asked for their mercy. Would they permit Joanna to live with them since he could not support her? "She is a talented weaver and is willing to work for you," he added.

Adah wondered, "How do I add a Canaanite woman who worships idols to our household?" And yet she could not refuse this connection with her lawless son. She ran to share the letter with Joel, who was working in the garden.

Fortress Antonia, Jerusalem

Roman power slowly became more firmly entrenched in Israel. Stories of merciless Roman cruelty, even death by crucifixion for minor offenses, circulated among the Jews. Joel and Adah observed more and more encroaching Roman rules and regulations in their little village.

The Roman rule established in Jerusalem staunchly maintained peace and order. It disturbed Joel and Adah to see the Roman militia stationed so near their beloved Jewish temple. Newly graduated centurions gathered for instructions at the Tower of Antonia, their military headquarters. The tower, which occupied a major portion of the sacred area of Mount Moriah, was originally built by the Macedonians to defend the temple. Herod recognized its strength and even connected it to the temple by a colonnade. Underneath this military garrison was a prison.

The centurions were elite Roman soldiers who had just been promoted to the rank of first level centurion after grueling training. They demonstrated potential leadership qualities.

The commanding centurion strode into the room and clapped his hands for attention.

"I am Commander Lucius Arias." He paused and studied his audience with an eagle eye. His superior air was irritating and demanding. "Because of your diligence and agility, you men of the Tiber are highly favored by the gods. But as centurions your allegiance must be to Caesar, who holds the greatest known power. The Greeks were the first to set mind above strength. The orator and philosopher were revered above the warrior. We Romans are also known among the nations for our poets, orators, and lawgivers. But the world knows the word *Roman* means master. You are here because Romans are masters of the sword. The world today presumes war is the eternal condition. So, devote yourself to war over mind and above God. You must commit your mind and body to Rome."

The chief centurion paused again, scrutinized his audience, and then tossed his patrician head for emphasis.

"You men were chosen for a special mission. Rome is usually at odds with the Jewish Sanhedrin, but today we have an unusual request from them. There is a new movement among the Jews with a leader from Galilee who claims to be God on earth," announced Lucius, his voice raised to impress. "You are aware that many troublemakers come out of Galilee. Jesus of Nazareth speaks Aramaic with a Galilean accent, Hebrew, and Greek. Many say that he heals the sick, raises the dead, cures the blind, and preaches a kingdom of love. His group is small but growing."

Lucius continued with cynicism. "The Jewish high priests are worried because Jesus claims to be their Messiah. He has preached to large crowds in Galilee. The high priests want us to watch him. I am dispatching each of you to the areas where he gathers crowds. I received news that he recently showed up in Judea. Marcus and Crispus, you are assigned to the Judean wilderness near the Jordan River. Find out what he tells people and how they respond. Then report back to me. If the Jews are disturbed about this man, the Romans need to find out his motives."

Lost and Found

Jeshur continued to scour the hills and valleys to the south and west, searching for Onam and the stolen sheep. Onam's theft had made life harder for all of the family, not to mention the shame he caused them.

Where is my wayward brother, and what has he done with my father's sheep? Jeshur wondered. A lifetime of investment and labor vanished overnight. At least Jeshur could trust Nathan with his own small flock while he was away.

The sun seemed to burn slowly across the brilliant blue sky. Dust covered Jeshur's face and cloak. He trudged over rocks and hills, carefully skirting deep ravines. At night, he usually found a small cave where he could sleep. The nights were veiled in the moon's luminous light. Occasionally Jeshur saw small flocks of sheep on the hills. He called his familiar call but received no response.

In his solitude, old memories sprang to mind as he walked along. He recalled the unforgettable sight of the angel's proclamation of the birth of the promised Messiah. Years ago, he and Nathan enjoyed telling about their experience of seeing the angels and the baby Jesus. But where was the peace the angel promised? There certainly wasn't peace on earth. Life had been a struggle for them all. He stopped telling the angel's story, even tried to push it out of his mind. Impossible.

Raising sheep and raising a family was hard work. He and his family barely managed to have enough to feed their children and raise their sheep. Onam's theft had made life even harder. The Romans' demand for taxes kept them struggling. How long would the Jews have to endure their Roman rulers? The angel's promise of goodwill to all people was now hard to believe.

Jeshur kept reminding himself that he had actually seen Jesus as a baby, but what had happened to him? Nathan and his father had also seen him.

Otherwise, Jeshur thought, it would be easy to think it had been a dream. Mary and Joseph seemed so genuine and trustworthy. What happened to them?

One morning Jeshur came upon a young shepherd herding his sheep. "I'm looking for my lost sheep," he explained. "Have you seen a big flock in this area lately?"

"Some time ago I saw two shepherds moving a flock to the northeast, toward the Jordan valley," the shepherd replied.

I haven't been that far, thought Jeshur. He thanked the young shepherd and headed toward the Jordan Valley, hoping to find his brother and the sheep. As he wended his way down a small canyon, he came to a shallow wadi. Sparse vegetation thickened into shrubs.

A welcome breeze poured across his path bearing a wave of sweet smells. What was that sound in the distance? A merry trickle of water running over stones from a crack in a cliff reminded him of the long-forgotten music of the angels. He welcomed the sight of the small stream and dropped to his knees, bathing his head in the cool water. It quenched his thirst and lifted his spirits. He followed the streambed lined with rough growth as far as the wilderness of Bethabarah. Among the distant trees ahead, he saw a crowd of people near springs of water. *They might have seen Onam and the sheep,* he thought. Drawing near, Jeshur observed their leader. He had unruly, sunburned hair and skin. He was dressed in a rough tunic of woven camel hair bound with a leather girdle. The leader admonished his captive audience to follow God's Son. He was careful to point out that they should not worship anyone but Jesus, the Lamb of God. The people listened closely.

Jeshur listened with interest; his search for Onam, forgotten. Then his heart skipped a beat as he heard the name Jesus. He hadn't heard that name since he had lived in his father's house. His mind suddenly flooded with memories of the angels and the baby Messiah.

Could this be Jesus, the Messiah I've wondered about for years? he thought.

The young preacher asked his audience to confess their sins and be baptized. He led a few of them out into waist-deep water. After baptizing them, he spied Jeshur standing on the bank.

"God be with you. My name is John," he said, wading out of the water. "Can I be of help?"

"I'm Jeshur, a shepherd from Bethlehem. Please, Rabbi, do you know where this man Jesus is? I would like to meet him."

"Yes, in fact I am his cousin, John." He bowed slightly and spoke as enthusiastically as the springs of water bubbling nearby. His eyes glistened in great excitement. "I was born first to announce his coming to earth, but I am not worthy to even untie his sandals. He is God's Son, and he came to tell all people how to have eternal life. Have you met him?"

John listened to Jeshur with great astonishment as the shepherd told his account of the angel's proclamation of Jesus's birth and how he and his brother saw Jesus the night he was born.

"You met him before I did!" exclaimed John.

"But he disappeared with Joseph and Mary many years ago, and we haven't heard anything about him since," recounted Jeshur. "For years I've wondered what happened to him."

"An angel came to my uncle Joseph one night in a dream warning the family to escape to Egypt. King Herod wanted to kill the baby," John explained. He lowered his voice because there were soldiers nearby. "Roman soldiers were sent to Bethlehem to find him. They killed many babies, hoping to kill him."

"Yes, they killed my little brother," Jeshur replied.

"How dreadful." John shook his head and sighed. "He still has many enemies who would like to kill him."

He glanced around. "But if you want to see Jesus, he is just near the Jordan River there." He gestured. "He won't be in Judea long, but I can tell you, he is all I live for. I live out here in the desert to tell people about him. He lives in Galilee but came to Judea to preach and baptize. His mother and some of his disciples are with him."

Jeshur was ecstatic. He hurried to the river to find Jesus. As he approached the throng of people, he noticed their eyes were riveted on a tall, slender man. He spoke with authority in a commanding voice. Jeshur listened with rapt attention.

> Suppose one of you has a hundred sheep and loses one of them. Does he not leave the ninety-nine in the open country and go after the lost sheep until he finds it? And when he finds it, he joyfully puts it on his shoulders and goes home.

Then he calls his friends and neighbors together and says, Rejoice with me; I have found my lost sheep. I tell you that in the same way there is more rejoicing in heaven over one sinner who repents than over ninety-nine righteous persons who do not need to repent.

Jeshur had never heard his rabbi preach with such authority. Jesus's words astonished him. It seemed as if Jesus was speaking directly to his heart. Nearby stood a group of women. Jeshur spotted Mary among them. She was older, but he still recognized her. After Jesus finished speaking, Jeshur approached her, greeting her by name. She turned, surprised, wondering how a stranger knew her name.

"I am a shepherd, Jeshur, son of Joel from Bethlehem. My brother and I first visited you in the cave behind the inn at Jesus's birth."

Mary looked at him in amazement. "Oh, your mother is Adah who was so kind to us when Jesus was a baby. My goodness, that was thirty years ago. I hope she is in good health. And you were such a wonderful family to visit us in Bethlehem. Come, you must meet Jesus." She led him through the dispersing crowd.

"Jesus, here is a shepherd who came to visit us when you were born in Bethlehem."

Jeshur's heart pounded as Jesus approached with outstretched arms. He was going to meet the Messiah, the Prince of Peace, the One whose birth was announced by angels.

Before Jeshur could bow, Jesus embraced him. "God be with you, Jeshur. And how is your father, Joel?" asked Jesus.

Jeshur groped for words and looked into Jesus's sparkling eyes. "He is well, sir. It would be a great honor if you could visit us while you are in Judea. I know my father would be glad to see you."

Jesus smiled, "God's blessing is with you. We will gladly come after we are finished here. John will come with us."

Jeshur was overwhelmed that he was having a conversation with the Messiah. Still, everyone was at ease in his presence. His features expressed a combination of intelligence, love, and depth of understanding. His voice was the voice of every man and yet beyond description. His actions were calm and deliberate. His dress was a full-sleeved undergarment reaching to his ankles and an outer robe of linen well exposed to the dust of the road.

"Jesus, I know you are the Messiah sent from God to give us peace as the angel announced, but I have many questions to ask about God and heaven," said Jeshur.

"If you have seen me, you have seen my Father. Do you believe that I am he?"

"Oh, yes, Rabbi, I do believe. But there is so much I don't know. The angels called you Lord, but where is your kingdom?"

"I am the way, the truth, and the life. Follow me and find the peace you seek." With that, Jesus led him into his heavenly kingdom and baptized him in the Jordan River. As Jeshur came up out of the water, he heard singing. "I hear music, but where is it coming from?" he asked, looking around.

Jesus replied, "Have you forgotten the angels' song? They sing and rejoice in heaven every time a sinner repents and believes."

Jeshur lingered two days more, drinking in Jesus's rich teachings. His heart burned as he heard how the heavenly Father cherished him, forgave him, and loved him beyond all measure. He left with the long-forgotten angels' song once again singing in his heart. He had found Jesus and had even entered his heavenly kingdom. The assurance of Jesus's incredible love for him changed his life completely. He strode home a new person, eager to share the good news of Jesus's coming visit.

Joel sat on a bench in his courtyard cleaning a goat skin. He looked up and saw Jeshur come in the gate. "Jeshur, welcome to the house of chaos," he greeted.

Jeshur asked, "What do you mean, Father?"

Joel led him inside, where his mother was busy churning. Tabitha was feeding a strange, childish-acting woman who moaned constantly. Tabitha's little girl sat on the floor crying. Their puppy yipped, running around the room. In another corner sat a pregnant foreign woman, weaving.

At the sight of Jeshur, his mother rushed to greet him.

"Jeshur, we were so worried," cried Adah. "You were gone for so long. We just received word that Onam is in jail. His wife brought us a letter from him. That's his wife, Joanna from Canaan. She's a weaver. She is living with us now." Jeshur looked around the room and shook his head.

"Mother," he interrupted, "I found Jesus and his mother, and they are coming for a visit in two days," said Jeshur.

"You found Jesus?" Adah asked incredulously. "Where?"

"While I was looking for Onam and the sheep, I found him preaching and baptizing over near the Jordan River. His mother asked about you," Jeshur added.

"Mary remembers me?" Adah's eyes widened with surprise. "So what happened to them when our babies were killed?"

"An angel warned them in a dream to leave Bethlehem before Herod's soldiers came," explained Jeshur. "They escaped to Egypt. After Herod died, they went back to their hometown. They live in Nazareth in Galilee. Joseph has died, so Mary travels with Jesus. His cousin, John, who is an evangelist, is coming with them."

"They are coming here … to see us?" Adah put her hand over her mouth and glanced at Madi and Joanna.

"Yes, in two days."

Adah began to wring her hands. "What will we do? We have nothing but a little goat cheese and a few vegetables."

"Mother, don't worry. I'll supply the roasted lamb from our flock and ask Hannah to come help you with all the preparations," Jeshur promised.

Adah's mind spun as she thought about preparing a feast for Jesus and his mother. "How do I prepare a dinner for a man whose birth was announced by angels?" she asked nervously.

"Don't worry, Mother. Hannah and I will help you," assured Tabitha.

Jeshur met Jesus, John, and Mary at the Bethlehem gate. Two Roman centurions discreetly followed at a distance. Jeshur took them by the inn and pointed out the cave at the back. "This is where you were born, Jesus. This is where we first saw you."

"Yes, I remember," whispered Mary. "It's just as I remembered, but it seems so long ago."

They followed the dusty road to their house, where Joel and the women waited anxiously.

Joel followed the traditional welcome to their home by saying, "Our home is your home."

Jesus put everyone at ease. "It is our pleasure to come. I am happy to meet the family that helped us when I was born. My mother has often told me of your generosity."

Jeshur turned to Adah. "Father wants to show Jesus and John the sheep pen out on the hill. Mary wants to visit with you. We'll be back by sundown."

The men, caught up in conversation, crossed the valley and climbed the hill.

"Here's where we were the night the angel announced your birth," said Joel. "The boys had just brought all the sheep in. We'd just finished our supper and settled down for the night."

Joel cleared his throat and leaned on his staff. "What a pleasure, after all these years, to meet the Messiah the angel told us about. It is a great honor for you to come back and visit the home of lowly shepherds. We lead a simple life. Here's the sheep pen my father built and where we always kept our flocks. I followed in his footsteps. He was the gate of the pen, and when he died, I became the gate."

Joel continued, "I love my sons who are to me what the temple was to Solomon. God gave me two sons who have done very well. I depend on Jeshur more, now that I'm old and Nathan is out on the neighboring hill there with our little flock. He has to keep moving them because the grass is sparse this time of year. But he also knows when they need to rest. I don't get out to the fields much anymore, but I can trust my sons to take good care of the sheep. I taught them where all the calm streams are and how to get the sheep safely across. They know how to guide them away from deep water."

Joel paused. "I have one son, Onam, who didn't want to be a shepherd." He shifted his weight and sighed.

"He left one night and took my whole flock with him." He paused, then continued. "Jeshur searched for them everywhere. Now we have a letter informing us that Onam's in jail." He shook his head. "I've always taught my sons how to protect the sheep from wolves, but I never thought of my own son stealing them."

He wiped his eyes and looked away.

"As the boys grew up, I gave each of them a ram's horn of olive oil to carry in case a sheep was wounded and a staff from that oak tree over there. I taught them how to protect our flock from wolves and jackals around here. And if a sheep strayed, I always looked for it until I found it. Once we lost a sheep: we couldn't find it for months. One day we stopped at a cave way up high on a hill to rest a bit, and there was that sheep on its back with its legs up in the air. Its wool was so heavy it couldn't walk! It took two of us to carry him back and shear off all that wool. It weighed nearly fifty pounds."

The men laughed.

"I'm an old man now." Joel paused and sighed. "But God has been good to me through the years. He's given me strength to keep working, a good family, a house to live in, and food to eat. Some day when I pass on, my land will belong to my sons."

Adah worried about how Madi and Joanna would react to their visitors, Madi with her unpredictable behavior and Joanna who worshiped Canaanite idols. Jesus's mother put them at ease with her soft, sympathetic voice.

When the men arrived, Jesus spoke with such kindness, all eyes focused on him. He greeted each member of the family as if they were his dearest friend. His mother brought wild, disheveled Madi to him. Jesus looked into her troubled eyes, took her hands, and said, "Peace I give you. Be healed."

The disheveled woman screamed and fainted. Adah tried to revive her. After a minute, she stirred and began weeping. She kissed Jesus's feet again and again.

"Thank you, dear Master and Lord. I'm healed! I am whole!"

Adah helped her up and beheld a new Madi.

Jesus spoke again. "Give thanks to the Lord for his unfailing love and his wonderful deeds, Mary. Give a sacrifice offering, and tell others of his works with songs of joy."

"Yes, my Lord," she sobbed. *He called me by my real name, Mary,* she thought. She looked around the room. Every eye stared at a woman so transformed it was hard to believe she was the same person. This deranged creature was now Mary of Magdala, smiling and happy. She danced around the room shouting, "I'm free! Praise God, I'm free. Adah, my sister. How nice to see you again. How long has it been since we were last together?"

Joanna came forward, knelt before Jesus, and gave him a gift of a finely woven seamless robe.

"The son of man thanks you," he said as he donned the robe. He took her hands. "The false gods you worship can never thank you. Your gift will always be remembered."

Joanna, overcome by his words, fell at his feet and kissed them.

"You are the God above all gods," she cried.

Madi was embarrassed, now that she was in her right mind. She had no gift to offer the one who had healed her.

"I have only thought about myself," she lamented, as she hung her head and wept.

Joel, embarrassed by the emotional scene, led the men to the courtyard.

"Jesus, we are humble shepherds who do not deserve your company, but please do the honor of blessing our food," Joel asked.

Jesus bowed his head and prayed, "Bless this home, this family, and the food that has been provided. May these shepherds ever be a blessing to further generations. May the truths they believe be a shining light in the darkness, leading others to the path of glory. Amen." Jesus's love for them seemed pure and warm and real. He broke the bread and passed it to the others as they reclined around the low table. They dined on a feast of roast lamb, bread, lentils, cheese, olives, figs, and grapes the women had prepared.

As was the custom at the end of the meal, Jesus gave a second blessing. At Jesus's invitation, the women gathered where they could hear.

"My father is also a shepherd," he said, looking at each one.

"My father is your father too. I lack nothing. He makes me lie down in green pastures, he leads me beside quiet waters. He restores my soul.

"He guides me in paths of righteousness for his name's sake.

"Even though I walk through the darkest valley, I fear no evil, for he is with me, his rod and staff, they comfort me."

Joel felt a pang of grief overlaid with peace.

Jesus picked up a cup. "You have prepared a table before me as my father has prepared a table before me in the presence of my enemies. He has anointed me with oil.

"My cup overflows.

"Surely goodness and love will follow me all the days of my life, and I will dwell in the house of the Lord forever."

Jesus paused. "I know you lost a son who died in my place. You will someday know how deeply I understand, and I too will be a sacrifice for all of you."

Adah caught her breath and looked at Jesus's mother, who bowed her head. All were deeply moved.

Jesus's visit, almost dreaded by Adah, ended too soon. Now she didn't want the group to leave. She and Tabitha, Madi, and Joanna stood at the gate watching Jesus, his mother, and John until they vanished out of sight. Jeshur went with them as far as the city gate and wished them God's journeying mercies on their way back to Galilee.

Two centurions also watched them leave. Marcus said, "You follow them, Crispus. I will stay here and see what these people are up to." They had already learned from village gossips that this family had "seen angels" and had a son in jail.

Jesus's visit left Joel's little house filled with joy. Adah felt an ecstasy she had never known. Madi went about humming, helping Tabitha and Joanna with the chores. Jesus's boundless grace had transformed their lives.

Nathan and Tabitha met a roadblock on their way to market the next morning.

"Where are you going?" asked a hard-faced centurion on horseback. He scrutinized them as if they had just committed a crime.

"My sister and I are going to the market, sir. She sells goat cheese there," explained Nathan.

"We're looking for a criminal in the area," the haughty centurion explained as Tabitha drew her veil over her face. "Have you seen any strangers here?"

"No sir," replied Nathan, respectfully. "I am Nathan and this is my sister, Tabitha, from the house of Joel." *Is the centurion referring to Onam?* he wondered.

"Someone said they saw visitors at your house recently," retorted the centurion.

"Jesus and his mother and his cousin John came for a visit. They left for Galilee yesterday," Nathan explained.

"Jesus? Who is he?" The centurion leaned forward. His gleaming armor shone brightly in the early morning sun. It was difficult to look at him. Tabitha studied the stones in the road as the men talked.

"Jesus is a rabbi, sir. He teaches and preaches the word of God," Nathan bravely replied. "He teaches people how to live peacefully with others."

"Does he say anything about soldiers?" asked the centurion.

"Oh, yes," Nathan replied. "Jesus said if a soldier asks you to carry his cloak for a mile, you should carry it two miles."

"Hmph! Here's my cloak. Carry it to the market for me." The centurion flung off his cloak and threw it to Nathan.

As they followed the centurion, Tabitha whispered to Nathan, "Is he looking for Jesus or Onam?"

Nathan and his sister joined the throngs in the market, relieved to be free of the centurion. Tabitha was glad to have a place under a tent to protect her cheese from the hot sun. Her regular customers came early because her cheese was a favorite at the market.

Nathan made his way down the stalls to see if his friend would sell some of his cured sheep skins.

"Do you come here often?" an articulate but demanding voice asked.

Tabitha looked up, her cheeks flushed, and her heart rose to her throat when she saw the centurion standing at her stall. She tried to hide her trembling hands. A little confused, she found her voice. "Yes, sir. I come nearly every day," she began. "Would you like a sample of my goat cheese?"

"Do you make this cheese yourself? It is very tasty," commented the centurion. His voice grew softer as he spoke.

"Thank you, sir." She lowered her eyes. "My mother taught me how to make it," she answered nervously.

"I have asked the villagers who they think Jesus is," the centurion said abruptly. "Many have never heard of him. Others think he's a fake when he claims to be God on earth. What do you think?"

"I know he is God's true son," replied Tabitha.

"How can you be so certain?"

"My father and brothers were out on the hillside many years ago when an angel suddenly appeared and told them Jesus, the Messiah, had been born here in Bethlehem. My brothers found him in the cave behind the inn with his mother and foster father just like the angel said. But his real father is God in heaven," she explained.

Now that Tabitha had seen and talked to Jesus, she suddenly felt a strength within herself to speak about him without fear. Jesus had convinced her beyond the shadow of a doubt that he was the Messiah.

"Did Nathan see the angels?"

"Oh yes, he saw them too."

"Do you believe your brother's story?" He looked at her intently.

"Of course." She lowered her eyes. This handsome centurion in his military uniform impressed her in spite of his offensive manner. Others began to notice the confrontation.

The centurion bowed slightly and left.

Tabitha's heart raced from being questioned in such a direct manner by a Roman centurion. Nathan sauntered up a few minutes later and noticed that her face was flushed.

"Let's go home, Nathan," she began, "Before that centurion decides to come back and ask more questions." She quickly gathered up her things and told her brother of her conversation with the centurion.

From time to time Tabitha and Nathan saw the centurion roaming around the market, Nathan was always on guard. One day the centurion approached them again, his voice kinder as he said, "Are you giving samples of your delicious cheese today?"

"I have tasty samples. Pick the one you like," Tabitha said, smiling nervously.

"You told me that you believe that the angel said Jesus is God's Son."

"Yes, that is true," Nathan intervened.

"But why are there so many gods? I see many people worshiping this god and that god."

"There are many false gods in the world," answered Nathan. "But the living God we worship is the creator of the world. God sent his Son, Jesus, to tell us about his love for us. He is the one true living God. He taught us not to worship anyone but him."

The centurion looked at Tabitha and said, "How do you know Jesus spoke the truth?"

"We saw him accept a gift from a Canaanite woman," answered Tabitha. "He said, 'the Son of Man thanks you. The gods you worship can never thank you.' False gods cannot speak or hear or even move. Jesus is the living God."

The centurion bowed, turned on his heel, and left.

Tabitha caught her breath, wishing the centurion knew the truth about God. How different he would act if he believed God loved him. His questions constantly disturbed her. His image impressed her, as if she were caught in an inescapable web, dangerous but delightful.

Atonement

Madi spoke up one evening as the family finished their supper. "I'm thankful for your care and for Jesus healing me. My life is fresh and my dreams are sweeter than they've ever been. You have accepted me as part of your family. But now that I'm well, I dream of returning home to Galilee."

Joel and Adah were surprised, but after some discussion, they felt that Madi was well enough to make the trip and care for herself. Adah reminded Joel that the Day of Atonement celebration at the temple in Jerusalem was approaching.

Joel hesitated. "This would be a good time for all of us to go to Jerusalem before the winter weather sets in. Jeshur can take Madi home after the festivities. My strength is limited and I feel aches and pains in my old bones, so I feel this may be my last trip."

Adah added, "I'm sure Joanna will want to visit Onam in prison."

Joel walked slowly, leaning on his shepherd's staff. Jeshur led the way with his wife, Hannah. Adah, Madi, Tabitha, and Joanna followed.

On their journey, Adah explained to Joanna how she came from a family of distinguished weavers. Her mother often recounted the story of how their ancestors had woven the veil that hung in the temple, thick as a man's hand. It concealed the holiest of holy rooms, which contained the ark of the covenant, Aaron's rod, and other items precious to the Jews. A chosen high priest entered on the Day of Atonement once a year to offer a blood sacrifice for the people's sins. Adah told them how her ancestors wove the blue, purple, and scarlet linen curtain, thirty feet wide and sixty feet long. They embroidered gold cherubim from the top to bottom. "It was a backbreaking and eye-straining task," she remembered her mother saying.

Adah lamented, "Even though my ancestors were recognized for their work, I will never be permitted to see it because women aren't allowed in the inner court."

The shofar sounded in the distance, calling people to worship.

"Our fathers loved this city," Adah exclaimed as the great gleaming temple came into sight.

"I wonder if Jesus will be there," said Madi as they joined throngs of people headed for the temple.

I wonder if I will see a certain centurion, dreamed Tabitha.

Tradition and festivity charged the air with expectation. As Joel and his family entered the gate of the magnificent building, they heard a familiar voice. That same voice had quickened their hearts and lifted their souls once before. Jesus stood on the steps of the temple and spoke to a gathering crowd of listeners. Joel and his family edged closer but were still far back in the crowd.

"Let me say this clearly," Jesus pointed out. "If a person climbs over or through the fence of a sheep pen instead of going through the gate, he's a sheep thief. The man who enters by the gate is the shepherd of his sheep. The sheep recognize his voice and follow him. They won't follow a stranger's voice but will scatter because they aren't used to the sound of it."

Jeshur glanced at Joel, who was listening intently.

"I am the gate for the sheep," Jesus continued. "All others are up to no good. They are sheep stealers. I am the Gate. Anyone who goes through me will be cared for. They will freely go in and out and find pasture. A thief comes there to steal and kill and destroy. I come so they can have real and eternal life, a better life than they ever dreamed of."

It sounds better than my miserable life, thought Joel.

Jesus continued. "I am the Good Shepherd. I know my own sheep, and my own sheep know me. In the same way, the Father knows me, and I know the Father. I put the sheep before myself, sacrificing myself if necessary. This is why the Father loves me: because I freely lay down my life. And so I am free to take it up again. I received this authority personally from my Father."

At that point the crowd began to murmur about Jesus's claims. But Joel brushed away a tear as he took the words of Jesus to heart.

I realize I must make peace with God and forgive Onam while I still have the chance, thought Joel. He turned to Adah. "We need to go see Onam while we are here."

"Are you sure you are ready?" Adah asked.

"Yes, by God's grace, I'm ready," Joel replied.

They left the temple and made their way to the dungeon. As they waited at the dungeon gate, prisoners came begging and crying for mercy. Some reached their hands through the bars, asking for food or water.

A guard approached. "What is your business here?" he asked sharply.

"Please grant me permission to speak to my son Onam," Joel answered.

The guard called another guard, who went inside calling for Onam. The guard returned, asking if Onam's wife was with them. "He only wants to see his wife," explained the guard. Joanna came forward while the rest of the family retreated to a distance, clutching each other in silence.

After a few minutes, Joanna came back with tears her eyes. "He's so ashamed for what he has done. He cannot face you," she explained. "He says you would never forgive him."

Adah embraced her while her own heart was breaking.

Joanna continued. "Onam says the judge will decide on his punishment soon. There is a possibility that he might be crucified."

"Crucified!" The family reeled at the thought of Onam dying by crucifixion.

Adah cried, "May God have mercy on our son."

Joel beat his breast, crying, "My son, my son, how we have all suffered! A great chasm has come between us that will never be moved. We will never understand one another." He pulled at his beard as they left.

Joel, shaken by the thought of Onam's death sentence, reflected on their way home to Bethlehem.

Life is a mixed blessing. I have been dealt both joy and misery. I am an eyewitness. I saw God's messenger tell of Jesus's birth, which I could not believe, and have even met Jesus personally. I've worked hard all these years and been blessed with a good family. Then I lost my baby son, killed by Roman soldiers who were looking for Jesus. I had a good flock of sheep and a good job selling them at the temple. I've followed the law and taught my children to follow in my footsteps. I provided a wife and flocks and land for my son and found a distant kinsman for my daughter to marry. I would have done the same for Onam, but he betrayed me, stealing my sheep and disappearing to goodness knows where. Now he faces the death penalty.

Throngs of people walked to and fro, busy with their own errands. It seemed that the whole world was passing him by.

Now, life has been hard, Joel thought. *The foreign wife of Onam came, bringing news that Onam is in prison. What shame he has brought to our family. But then Jesus came for a visit and understood how I felt. His Father is a shepherd too. He blessed our family and baptized my eldest son, Jeshur. He healed Adah's deranged cousin. Who could do that but God? He accepted Joanna's gift even when she was a pagan Canaanite. I forgive Onam,* he concluded, *and Jesus has given me peace.*

Recalling Jesus's words, Joel quickened his step. Jesus had told Joel's family that he was the Good Shepherd. When a lost sheep was found, he celebrated. Joel realized that he had indeed been a lost sheep. No one but Jesus could change his attitude. No one but God could do that.

"Jesus is God on earth, and this lost sheep has been found," he announced.

Soft summer breezes surrendered to autumn's crisp air. Every whisper of wind seemed colder than usual to Joel. Adah watched his painful gait with sadness. Joel managed to harvest hay for the sheep and crops for his family with the help of his sons. His aches and pains made him realize that he was growing older. The shadowy realization that he would one day die crept into his mind. In spite of his brave actions, his shoulders sagged under the added sheepskin cloak he wore to warm his weary body. Finally his painfully slow steps came to a halt, his eyes dimmed, and his mind dreamed of the past. He was a boy once again in his father's home. He remembered his father building their little house of stone and mortar. It was small but sturdy and accommodated their family of six children, Joel being the eldest.

In his dreams, he ran and played games with his brothers and took his turn guarding the sheep. Then there was his bride, Adah, as sweet as a fresh flower. The lambs and babies came, increasing his responsibilities. He and his family dutifully followed the Torah as their parents had taught them. They tried to follow all the requirements of the law, teaching their children to repeat the Shema every morning and night so by age twelve they could repeat it for themselves.

Hear, O Israel; the Lord our God, the Lord is one, Love the
Lord your God with all your heart, with all your soul and
with all your strength. (Deuteronomy 6:4-5).

And then he met Jesus, a man who was greater than the law they had
always followed. Jesus told people to love God and love others as themselves.
Joel had never thought of God as a loving God, but suddenly he realized
that God loved him beyond all measure!

*God loves me, even though I am a poor shepherd, even though my body is old
and my mind is feeble. He will not love me any less for that,* he mused. *When
will I see his face?*

Joel still wondered where Jesus's kingdom was. If the Jews were God's
chosen people, why did they have to struggle so to make a living? Why did
some Jews disregard the Torah, marry pagans, and worship idols, forsaking
the God of their forefathers? Now, since he had met Jesus, all of these things
seemed to be of little consequence. Jesus gave him assurance that he would
one day join him in heaven and that was all that mattered. He sighed and
fell asleep as he often did on a soft pile of sheep skins.

A Time to Live and a Time to Die

Nathan led the lambs to new sprigs of grass. The sheep helped themselves to patches of fragrant herbs, all encouraged by recent spring rains. Up the slopes, the full-horned rams rummaged on the tough weeds that sprang up among the rocks. Jeshur oversaw the garden near his father's home while Tabitha and Joanna spent time helping Adah take care of their ailing father.

One balmy day in the midst of spring's promise of new life, Joanna's birth pangs began. Tabitha ran to fetch the midwife, who arrived soon with her birthing stones. Adah and Tabitha massaged her back and encouraged her as the midwife delivered a healthy baby boy.

"He looks just like Onam," exclaimed Adah. Tabitha ran to tell her father the good news while Adah reveled in her new grandson.

Joel nodded and smiled. "God is good," he murmured weakly, grasping her hand. "Tabitha, I must speak with Nathan."

"Yes, Father," she whispered. "He will be here tonight." She bowed and laid her cheek against his head.

As they finished their evening meal, Nathan knelt by his father's bed. "Father, you wish to speak to me?"

"My concern is for Joanna," confided Joel in a husky voice. His labored breathing slowed his speech. "She is a good woman, and even though she is Canaanite, she has become one of us. We know Joanna has no future with Onam. We realize that his life and mine will soon end. Make sure that she and her baby are cared for."

"I promise to take care of them, Father," said Nathan. He held his father's leathered face in his hands and kissed him.

"The nights make this old man grow lonelier," groaned Joel, clasping his son's hand. "I don't want you to ever feel such loneliness."

"Don't worry. Just rest," Nathan whispered. He loved his father deeply and ached to think of losing him. His mind flooded with memories of his father's wisdom as he watched him fall asleep.

Adah asked Jeshur to call the family together the next morning to bid their father goodbye. Children and grandchildren surrounded his bed. Joel spoke faintly.

"I love each of you as I love my own body. I have not always been the easiest man to live with, but I want you to know that I love you." He paused and looked at Adah, who took his trembling hand.

"You have been a good and wise husband and father," she said as she bent down and stroked his forehead.

"I wish Onam were here," he continued. "My only regret is that I failed to listen to him. And I regret losing my Ezer, that sweet baby of ours." He paused and wiped his eyes.

Joanna spoke up. "Father, Onam's son is here. I have named him 'Ezer-Joel' for you and your baby son. We will never forget you."

She brought the baby to him for his blessing, Nathan by her side. Joel smiled and blessed them. Then he blessed each child and grandchild one by one, admonishing them to be faithful to the Lord and to each other. He gazed at Adah for a moment, closed his eyes, and in a few minutes slipped away.

"I cannot believe my father has died," wailed Tabitha, kneeling at his side.

Wailing continued throughout the day while they bathed the family patriarch's body, wrapped it in linen cloths, and carried it to the cemetery on the shoulders of his sons and grandsons.

Adah explained to the mourners who came to grieve with her, "We buried him with great dignity, following the Jewish rituals passed down from generation to generation. And yet, it was different because I was burying my husband and my children's father."

Adah and Tabitha, dressed in sackcloth, retreated to their home after Joel's funeral. They sat silently in the gathering darkness, refusing food or a lighted oil lamp. Tabitha, widowed by the loss of her own husband, keenly felt the clutches of sorrow when her father died.

She turned to her mother. "I can't explain it," she whispered, "but I felt death move into our house like a dark shadow when Papa was dying. I was numb with fear and self-pity."

"Your father was very ill," Adah said, sighing. "You wouldn't want him to continue suffering, would you? Death comes to us all." She looked away and brushed tears from her cheeks.

"Tabitha, we don't know what the future holds, but God does. Look, he has given you a beautiful little daughter. You must think of her. And you have your memories of Papa. And I have you, Jeshur, and Nathan to help me. I have so much to thank God for. Let's light the lamps and rid our house of the dark shadows."

Tabitha embraced her mother. "You are so strong," she cried.

The next morning Adah scurried around preparing breakfast. "Come, Tabitha, let's grind the wheat and milk the goats. I hear them calling. We need to prepare cheese to take to the market."

As Nathan and Tabitha made their way to the market, many friends and neighbors expressed their condolences. The siblings were impressed by how much people respected their father.

The centurion spied them, got off his horse, and made his way over to their stall. "I have not seen you at the market for some time," he said.

Nathan explained that their father had died and they were unable to attend to their business.

"I am sorry to hear of your father's death," replied the centurion.

"I have also received news that Jesus's cousin, John, who visited you, was jailed because he criticized King Herod. He was recently beheaded."

Tabitha gasped, and Nathan shuddered in disgust.

"Please be careful what you say," continued the centurion. "There are many listening ears." With that, he left.

After a challenging day at the market, Tabitha and Nathan walked home in silence and grief, remembering Jesus's and John's visit to their home. Tabitha suddenly stopped. "I remember when I was a little girl, Mother and I visited Mary in the cave when Jesus had just been born. She told us the story of her cousin Elizabeth who was going to have a baby. That baby was John, who came to announce the coming of Jesus. How could this happen to him? Poor Elizabeth and Zechariah." She sighed. "John was a brave man."

How will this effect Jesus's ministry now that John is not there to help him? Nathan wondered.

Good News Is Bad News

Lucius Arias strode into Fortress Antonia and acknowledged the men's salute. "We have gathered you here today for your reports on the movement among the Jews and their leader, Jesus of Nazareth." His crisply spoken words sharpened the men's attention. "Marcus, what did you find out in the Judean wilderness?"

"There are people who believe in Jesus, sir, especially a family of shepherds who claim an angel told them about his birth in Bethlehem. They believe he is God. However, many others doubt their story. Jesus has become somewhat popular, speaking to greater and greater crowds of people and baptizing them. He has a following of twelve men and a number of women who are very committed followers. I don't see any evidence of his starting a rebellion. I learned that his disciple, John the Baptist, was recently imprisoned when he criticized King Herod and later beheaded."

Crispus spoke up. "The Jewish priests and Pharisees despise Jesus because he doesn't teach their beliefs. They are jealous of his popularity and question the miracles he performs. They are fearful that people will forsake worshiping at the temple to follow Jesus. They would lose their business at the temple market. I think they are looking for a way to get rid of him, even by crucifixion."

"Convince someone to publicly accuse him of something, anything," suggested Lucius. "How dedicated are his followers? Surely there is one of them who could be persuaded to help us. We might even offer a small reward."

"I have a suggestion," said Crispus. "Jesus has become more popular by pretending to raise a friend from the dead. The leading Pharisee informed me that he and other Pharisees will attend a dinner at the home of Lazarus, the man Jesus 'raised from the dead,' tomorrow night. Jesus is also invited. We'll surround the house and capture him there. It will be easy since the Pharisees who are guests will be eyewitnesses. The other unsuspecting guests won't be able to defend him."

The evening air was refreshed by a short spring shower. Nocturnal creatures croaked their tunes. Lamp light flickered and danced around Lazarus' and Martha's courtyard, enhancing the surroundings.

Lazarus, some Pharisees, and Jesus and his disciples dined in the courtyard. They tried to ignore the crowd outside the gate gawking at Lazarus, back from the dead. Martha's sister, Mary, came out of the house with a bottle of expensive perfume and walked straight to Jesus. She knelt and poured the perfume on his feet while the men watched in surprise. Mary didn't care who was watching. She cried so hard her tears fell on his feet. She loosened her braids and wiped his feet with her hair. To the men's surprise, Jesus greeted her warmly.

The boisterous laughter died to a murmur. The sweet odor of exquisite perfume filled every nostril. Jesus helped Mary to her feet. She turned and ran back to the kitchen, while the guests gaped in astonishment.

"Who was that woman?" asked a Pharisee.

Jesus explained, "Leave her alone. This gift has anointed me for my death."

The men began to speculate with each other, trying to understand what they had just witnessed.

Judas, a disciple of Jesus, exclaimed, "Why did this woman waste an expensive jar of perfume on Jesus when it could have been sold to help some poor family?"

The Pharisees began to murmur among themselves in agreement.

Among the bystanders outside the gate were centurions dressed in disguises, ready for action.

"Wait," signaled Crispus. "See that man who complained about wasting the perfume on Jesus? Let's talk to him. He may be the very man we need to help us." The centurions faded into the darkness. Crispus lingered, waiting for Judas.

Punishment

While Nathan helped Tabitha at the market, they noticed a huddled group of people at the next stall getting the latest news. Humpback Rhoda, the town gossip, sauntered over and pointed a finger at Tabitha. It was often rumored her hoarse cackle and bad breath could wake the dead!

"Say, aren't you the wife of the man who sees angels?" she asked with a toothless grin.

Tabitha caught her breath. "I'm his sister, if that's what you mean."

"Don't you have a brother in jail?" the woman squinted her eyes.

Tabitha, grimacing, replied that she did.

"I thought so." Rhoda took a step closer and looked around, eager to share her news.

"I don't know if you heard, but your brother is going to be crucified just before Passover."

Tabitha almost fainted, but Nathan caught her. They couldn't believe their ears.

At that moment Marcus, the centurion, rode up and dismounted. "Tabitha, Nathan, I have bad news for you. Your brother who is in jail will be crucified before Passover. He has been charged with insurrection and thievery. I tried to speak to him, but he wouldn't talk." Marcus touched her hand, bowed, and left.

"Hurry. We must go tell Jeshur," said Nathan. "We must try to save Onam from the cruelest kind of death."

Jeshur, on hearing their news, exclaimed, "There's nothing I can do. Onam's punishment brings shame to our family. We must be strong and put our faith in God."

Nathan persuaded Jeshur to go to Jerusalem to support their brother as he faced death.

"Let's go by cover of night," suggested Jeshur. "I don't want to meet friends who will question us."

The cloak of darkness fell heavy on their shoulders. The morbid air depressed them. Their minds dwelt on the terrible consequences concerning their doomed brother, limiting their conversation.

A nearly full moon rose secure in its orbit, set in place by its creator. It silently, relentlessly pushed back the darkness that tried to conquer the earth. The moon's creator also stood secure in his position as evil men planned to snuff him out as if he were just another annoying human being. He didn't fit into their plan of conquest.

Why are they planning this crucifixion just before Sabbath Passover? Jeshur wondered.

He was grateful for the moonlight that spread over the peaceful hillsides. They passed by the villages where smoldering cooking fires wafted through the night air. Families slept secure, trusting in God, who heard his own Son crying out for protection while his trusted friends slept nearby under an olive tree.

A glow on the distant eastern horizon announced the coming sunrise in all its beauty and perfection, the sun that sustained life on earth. Watching the sunrise roused fear within the brothers' hearts. That very day the sun would be overcome by darkness as dark as the evil in imperfect men's hearts. Israel's religious leaders sought that which was evil, but in their eyes, it looked so good. A rooster crowed in the distance, announcing the dawn and a betrayal. Jeshur and Nathan quickened their steps in spite of the fatigue that besieged them. They threaded their way through the maze of temporary shelters of pilgrims who had traveled from near and far to celebrate the Passover feast.

Sunlight danced on the tall spires of the temple in Jerusalem—the temple, where Jeshur and Nathan saw Jesus teach people to love and trust each other. Their eyes scanned the Gentiles' court, the women's court, the court of men, then, on to the inner court, containing the holy of holies, infinitely sacred, infinitely beautiful.

"One day my youngest son, Johnathan, will soon be old enough to come with us to the Feast of the Passover," Jeshur commented.

They pressed on through throngs of people opening their shops, going about their daily affairs; bargaining with customers. It seemed like just another ordinary day. They stopped at the market long enough to buy the necessary burial garments for Onam, shuddering at the grim necessity. The shopkeeper keeper offered his condolences. "When did your brother die?" he asked.

I hope we can see Jesus when this is all over. I'm sure he will be here somewhere, thought Nathan, his feelings sinking. *He gives me such reassurance. Maybe his mother will be here too. I hope Mother and Joanna don't hear about Onam's crucifixion since they are visiting Mary Magdalene in Bethany.*

The men edged their way through the crowded streets and climbed Mount Golgotha, the place of the skull. They entered the site of their brother's crucifixion with heavy hearts and numbly scanned the stage of execution, where men die a slow, torturous death. There were three heavy wooden posts laid side by side.

Who are the others to be crucified, and why are the Jewish leaders here? Jeshur wondered.

"Why is the Sanhedrin here?" asked Nathan, puzzled.

The Sanhedrin, dressed in their high turbans, long white robes, and blue prayer shawls, signified outstanding wisdom and purity in their own eyes. They sat in prominent seats near the front of the crowd to be seen by the people and to assure that justice was carried out.

A blast of trumpets announced a parade of soldiers. An ominous drum cadence followed, causing the crowd to fall back in awe. The soldiers' dramatic entry enforced Rome's authority by their armor, shields, and spears. Centurions, following on horseback, demonstrated Roman strength and conquest. Next came the event for which the lawless crowd was waiting. The first convict, bent under a heavy crossbeam, slowly struggled in.

"Crucify him!" cried the crowd. Their burst of raucous laughter unnerved Jeshur.

"Look, that's Onam," gasped Nathan.

The brothers almost didn't recognize their once-handsome brother, Onam, accompanied by soldiers goading him on with their whips like a wild animal in the gruesome parade. His once-muscular body was now unbelievably lean and gaunt. A burst of pity mixed with revulsion filled the brothers' hearts as they watched their little brother strain under his heavy load. As Onam passed by, the cries of the callous crowd looking for entertainment escalated to hooting and shouting. Jeshur flinched when he saw him and buried his head in his hands as he heard his own brother scream in pain.

Merciless Roman soldiers attached his crossbeam to one of the posts, then hammered his wrists and feet to the cross. Unceremoniously they hoisted Onam, writhing on his cross, dropping it with a thud into its hole. Onam screamed again. His face was black and blue, and his body showed extreme whiplash marks. Jeshur and Nathan gasped to see such a display of Roman cruelty.

Another criminal arrived carrying his heavy beam. He seemed somewhat older. More screams of agony as rough Roman hands nailed him to a cross. The crowd feasted on the display of blood and cruelty.

A third man in the parade who, with the aid of a large man, struggled to carry his cross beam, his beaten, bloody body too spent to carry it alone. A sharp thorn branch twisted into a bloody wreath crowned his brow.

"He must be the worst criminal," Jeshur said, shuddering. "I wonder who he is. What was his crime?"

Screams of agony rose above the crowd's fevered chanting as the third man was nailed to a cross and positioned between the other two criminals.

One of the soldiers climbed a ladder and nailed a sign above his head. It read, "JESUS OF NAZARETH, THE KING OF THE JEWS."

Jeshur's heart stood still. He felt rooted to the ground. No one heard his soundless scream. Nathan was stunned beyond words.

Jesus, the one whose birth had been announced by angels, the one who had taught their family to love one another, the one who had baptized Jeshur, now hung dying on a cross like a common criminal.

"This is a ghastly mistake! This cannot be Jesus!" Jeshur finally exploded.

A man standing nearby sneered, "It's him, all right. He was a slick one, but they finally got him."

"But what was his crime?" asked Jeshur with agitation.

"They say he was leading a rebellion."

"But this man is the Son of God," retorted Jeshur, still reeling from shock.

"Oh, yes, he claimed to be God on earth. A lot of men make that claim. Aren't we all sons of God? If he's God, why doesn't he come down from that cross? He's a fake and deserves to die. He was beginning to have the wrong kind of influence on people." The man spat on the ground and left.

"What can we do to stop this execution?" cried Jeshur, searching the senseless crowd for help. "I know it's hard to see my own brother crucified, but this just cannot be happening to Jesus. He's the innocent Son of God."

The callous mob jeered and laughed, applauding the cruel scene.

Jeshur spied Jesus's mother coming through the crowd, leaning on Mary Magdalene's arm, his own mother and Joanna, heavy with grief. Jeshur and Nathan made their way through the crowd to comfort them.

"I hoped you wouldn't come. How did you find out about Onam?" Jeshur asked his mother.

"Joanna heard the news at the market this morning," said Adah. "We felt that we had to come."

"My heart is crushed with shame for Onam," Jeshur exclaimed, "but they are crucifying Jesus too!" The women gasped as they viewed the ghastly scene and clung to each other.

"Someone has made a terrible mistake! We must stop this execution. It's a horrible injustice!" continued Jeshur. They joined the little band of Jesus's followers.

John, one of Jesus's disciples who accompanied the women, shook his head. He spoke sorrowfully. "Early this morning I slipped into the courtyard and spoke to the high priest, an acquaintance of mine, but he wouldn't listen. It's a political move. The Jewish officials and the Roman soldiers arrested Jesus and took him to Pilate, the governor. Rome sent Pilate to govern Judea because they couldn't find anyone else for the job. Pilate is inflexible. He rules with a heavy hand. He always comes to Jerusalem during Passover celebration in case he needs to quell an uprising. He is a spiritually blind pagan. All he cares about is maintaining peace in Jerusalem."

"But this is a Jewish matter. Why have they brought Jesus to Pilate?" asked Jeshur. "He has no jurisdiction over a Jewish religious matter."

"That's right. They made me leave when I pointed that out, so there was nothing I could do," John agreed. "The truth is, the high priests were jealous of Jesus and wanted to get rid of him. He faced trumped up charges by the Jewish officials. The Romans didn't like the fact that he claimed to be a king and talked about his kingdom. It was a sham of a trial. Nobody could come up with solid charges against him. It's a senseless execution in every way."

The sun climbed higher, intensifying the pain and agony of the three dying men. Buzzards flew in circles with great expectation, attracted by the bloody scene, while flies and gnats enjoyed a banquet at the expense of the criminals. The gruesome sight of suffering swelled the empty crowd to a fevered pitch. Even the chief priests and teachers of the law joined in.

"He saved others, but he can't save himself. Come down from the cross, and we will believe you, King Jesus," they scoffed.

Jeshur, numb with agony, spoke to Mary. "Jesus is all that I ever hoped for. He told me to believe in him. How can I trust him when he is dying? Yet, if he dies, I believe his love will live forever."

Nathan saw the Roman soldiers gambling over Jesus's clothing. There was Joanna's seamless robe she had woven for him, spattered with blood. The soldier who won it in a craps game stuffed his prize in his pouch. Joanna burst into tears remembering how Jesus had forgiven her when he accepted her gift.

Jesus spoke with a strained voice, "Father, forgive them. They do not know what they are doing."

The soldiers howled with fiendish laughter.

Onam raised his head and saw his brothers and mother.

"We're here. We forgive you," shouted Jeshur.

"I love you all," cried Onam in agony. When he saw Joanna, he hung his head and wept. He called to the other criminal, "That's my family, Lud."

"That is Jesus beside you," called Jeshur. "He loves you."

Onam gasped and looked at Jesus. He remembered his family visits with Joseph and Mary and the baby Jesus. He had heard wonderful things about him since then from his family, but what had he done to die like a criminal?

Lud, squirming in agony, called out, "If you are the Messiah, then save yourself and save us too."

"Shut up, Lud," said Onam. "We deserve our punishment, but I've heard about this man all my life. He came to save us, but I listened to you instead. Jesus is the Son of God. Jesus, I'm sorry I never believed you, but please forgive me and take me with you to your kingdom."

Lud scoffed. "You're making a big mistake believing him. If he's God, why is he going through all this miserable punishment?"

"I believe in you, Jesus," repeated Onam, gasping for breath.

"I will take you with me to paradise today," promised Jesus. "I am the lamb of God dying to forgive your sins and the sins of the whole world."

Onam felt the scales of his unbelief fall away. The awful burden of his crime lifted, and light swirled through his soul. Joanna and Adah knelt at the foot of his cross weeping until soldiers pulled them away.

Jesus turned to Onam, his voice hoarse and strained. "Peace be with you."

Jeshur, not able to control his emotions, yelled at the crowd, "This is an innocent man who's being crucified. He's not a criminal."

People nearby turned and stared. Others laughed and jeered.

"That's what they all say!" someone hooted. Jeshur turned around hopelessly. He spotted two centurions on horseback at the back of the crowd.

"You stay here with the women, Nathan. I'll see if we can stop this crucifixion." He pushed his way back to the centurions, dressed in all their regalia. They sat with arms folded in seemingly cold-blooded detachment. They had observed this scene a thousand times.

Jeshur pled, "You've got to stop this execution. I've known Jesus from the day he was born. He was sent by almighty God to bring peace to the world and to teach people how to love one another."

"He broke the law and deserves to die," shouted Crispus. The other centurion dismounted and walked with Jeshur through the crowd. Crispus shouted in a shrill voice, "Come back, Marcus! You don't want to get mixed up with those narrow-minded Jews." He ground his teeth as he watched his companion follow Jeshur through the crowd.

Jeshur shouted, struggling with emotion, "You see that woman." He pointed out Mary Magdalene. "She was demon possessed. She lived with our family for a month. She nearly drove us all crazy. Jesus came for a visit and healed her. And there's Jesus's mother, Mary. She can tell you about Jesus's miraculous birth. When she was a virgin, an angel told her she would give birth to God's Son who would come to save us from our sins." They edged through the mocking mass to the foot of the cross. The centurion looked up and came to a sobering awareness of the Son of God's divine agony.

"John," called Jesus.

The crowd hushed to hear what he would say as John came forward and called out, "What is it, Lord?"

"Take my mother home with you."

"Yes, Lord. Our home is hers as long as she lives."

Mary was touched by his words. *In spite of all his agony, he remembers that after Joseph died, I sold our house to contribute to his work and follow him. He knows I have nowhere to go.*

Jesus spoke in a loud voice, "Father, why have you rejected me?" The troubled sky grew dark and still.

"I'm thirsty," he whispered faintly.

The centurion barked, "Get him some wine. Put it on a sponge." A soldier tied a sponge to a spear, dipped in wine and gall, and lifted it to Jesus. He tasted the bitter mixture and refused it. "It is finished," he said. He bowed his head and breathed his last.

Out in the desert, dust-filled clouds, whipped by a moaning wind, turned black. A low rumble escalated to a crescendo of thunder followed by lightning. The panicking crowd, peppered by rocks and dust, stumbled around in the darkness. They cried and beat their breasts in the blinding rain that followed. The Sanhedrin joined the crowd sloshing through mud puddles mingled with the blood of criminals that spattered the fringes of their priestly robes. Their job was finished. Justice had been done. No more having to deal with the man who claimed to be God. They ran, careful not to step on Gentile ground, making them unclean even though they carried Jesus's blood on their sacred prayer shawls. They hurried to preside over the main event of the day, the Passover Sabbath meal.

Most of the elite guard, led by Crispus, took off on their horses, leaving Marcus, the other centurion, alone. Marcus, observing the elements of nature demonstrating God's fury, knelt at the cross and cried out, "Surely this man was the Son of God."

The Sanhedrin had requested Pilate to finish the crucifixion. They had to preside over the Passover Sabbath celebration that evening commemorating the first Passover meal.

In the temple, a handwoven veil hiding the Holy of Holies was torn from top to bottom. Because of his love for them, God opened the way for people everywhere to come to him without going through a human priest.

The wind died to a whimper, and the rain diminished to a few sprinkles. A faint, eerie light dawned on the ghastly scene.

Jeshur and Nathan watched the remaining soldiers break Onam's and

Lud's legs. They screamed, writhed in pain, and quickly died. Another soldier, seeing Jesus had already died, and as an afterthought, turned back, drew his spear, and pierced Jesus's side for good measure. He was unaware that he fulfilled the last of a string of ancient prophecies concerning Jesus's death. Water and blood gushed from his lifeless body. Mary and Adah, who had just lost their sons, wailed and clutched each other, sobbing and beating their breasts. Mary remembered Simeon's prophecy when they first took Jesus to the temple for his dedication: "Your own heart will be pierced."

The women gathered around Mary, in utter hopelessness at the cross, their clothes soaked to the skin. Grief owned the day.

Mary's tears mingled with the raindrops. *How could Jesus's life end so tragically? I always believed in him. Now I've lost him. My life is meaningless without him. And yet, my soul still praises the Lord, and my spirit rejoices in God my Savior, for he has been mindful of the humble state of his servant.*

But how shall we bury him? Will my son, the King of Kings, be buried in a common pauper's grave and forgotten? Where are Jesus's disciples who committed their lives to follow him to the end? A king in a pauper's grave? Well, after all, he was born in a lowly cave. Jesus said he was going to paradise today and take Onam, Adah's son, with him. That is what we will hope for.

An elderly woman with a walking stick hobbled up to Mary. "You probably don't recognize me, Mary. I am Abigail, the innkeeper's wife who delivered Jesus. You told me when he was born he was the Messiah sent from God. Some God he was. Well, because of you I lost my husband when those Roman soldiers killed all the babies in Bethlehem. They forced me to tell them where all the babies lived that I had delivered. Then they killed them, hoping to kill Jesus. They killed my husband too, when he tried to protect me. My son, Lud, was crucified with your son today. Lud and I had to flee Bethlehem for our lives, and it's all your fault. We could hardly keep ourselves alive living in Jerusalem.

"I remember those three wealthy Persians who brought you rich gifts. Everybody in Bethlehem knows how you ran off with all that wealth. You must have lived a life of ease all these years. And see how Jesus's claim to be God ended? He just stirred up trouble. At least my Lud got revenge for his father's murder. I showed him the soldier who killed his father. An eye for an eye and a tooth for a tooth, I always say."

Mary looked away, and said nothing.

Adah could not keep silent any longer. "Abigail, I'm Adah from Bethlehem. You delivered two of my babies, Onam and Ezer. Those soldiers who killed your husband killed my Ezer too. It was all your fault. I forgive you because Jesus taught us how to forgive and how to love each other. I believe Mary when she says Jesus is ... or was the Messiah. An angel told her she would be the mother of the Messiah. My husband and two sons saw the angel announce his birth while they were out on a hill with their sheep. My sons saw him in the cave."

"Yes, I remember seeing them. I was still there with Mary," recalled Abigail.

"Jesus and Mary blessed us with a visit not long ago," continued Adah. "He blessed us all and healed my insane cousin before our eyes. I'm not blaming you for Onam's choosing to follow Lud. That was his choice. My husband and I did everything we could to teach our son God's laws. Thank the Lord Onam asked Jesus to forgive him on the cross."

"That's nonsense," retorted Abigail. "Only God in heaven can forgive sins."

Adah continued, "You planted seeds of hatred in Lud's heart that led him to kill that soldier regardless of the reason. Then he got Onam involved and stole all our sheep. Here is Joanna, Onam's wife. She came to live with us, and even though she is Canaanite, she no longer worships her Canaanite gods. She believed in Jesus too." Adah continued. "My husband died not long ago. I've found that widowed life is hard. I'm sorry for your loss and your son's crucifixion, but I heard Jesus say he was taking Onam with him to paradise, and I believe him. I believe everything he taught was the truth. I'm sorry you never knew him."

Abigail backed away. "I ... need to go bury my son," she muttered.

"And we need to bury ours," said Adah, breaking into tears.

Mary Magdalene stood weeping at Jesus's cross with bowed head. She shuddered at the unthinkable scene, now permanently etched in her mind. She turned to John. "I cannot believe that my Lord is dead. He gave us all such hope. How can we go on without him? What shall we do? Where shall we bury him?

John answered, "We need to buy a shroud and spices, but Judas has the money bag. I wonder where he went."

"Many of Jesus's followers ran away when the storm broke," said Mary Magdalene, surveying the retreating crowd.

The clouds slowly gave way to the sun's radiance, which lifted their spirits. There was an unexplained calm in the air.

"Look," said Mary Magdalene. A brilliant rainbow arched in the heavens, framing the three crosses, a symbol of God's promised covenant with Israel. The three crucified men were washed clean, their wounds more prominent; Jesus's crown of thorns was torn away.

Two men approached and took Jesus's body down from the cross. They introduced themselves to the women as Nicodemus and Joseph of Arimathea. Mary knelt by Jesus's body, kissed his forehead, and whispered, "My son and my Savior." She caressed his wounded hands, remembering when his infant fingers had clutched her hair.

"Mary, Nicodemus and I have been secret followers of Jesus," explained Joseph. "We have Pilate's permission to bury him. May we also have your permission? It would be an honor to place him in our new family tomb. It's in a garden not far from here."

"You are most kind. We appreciate your help," said John. Joseph led them to a garden where only the wealthy buried their dead. John and the women followed.

Joseph and Nicodemus wrapped Jesus's body in a linen sheet, using spices fit for a king, and laid him in the tomb. They rolled a large stone across the opening to seal it. By then the sun was low in the sky.

Three crosses

"It's getting late. We'll come back after the Sabbath to finish the burial," Mary Magdalene promised Mary. Meanwhile Roman soldiers gathered to guard Jesus's sealed tomb.

Jeshur and Nathan took Onam's body down from his cross. Marcus, the centurion, took off his armor and left it with his sword and shield at the foot of Jesus's cross.

"Let me help you," he insisted. "My name is Marcus."

"Aren't you the centurion we've talked to at the Bethlehem market?" asked Nathan.

"Yes, I recognized you when I saw you at Jesus's cross," Marcus replied. "In Bethlehem I didn't understand how you believed that Jesus was God on earth."

The men wrapped Onam's body while Joanna clung to Adah for support.

"Look," said Adah. "Abigail left Lud hanging on the cross."

"I'll take care of him," said Marcus. He took Lud's body down and wrapped it in his own cloak.

"You're a centurion. Why are you helping us?" asked Jeshur.

"Now I know that Jesus was truly the son of God. He has given me the peace I've searched for all my life," replied Marcus.

At the cemetery, the three men worked quickly, digging two graves in the growing dusk, defying the Passover hour. The afternoon rain had mercifully softened the soil.

"Thank you for taking care of Onam. I am glad to know where he's buried," cried Joanna. They turned to leave but were startled to see a dead man lying nearby.

"That's Judas," exclaimed Marcus. "He was the follower of Jesus who betrayed him into the hands of the Jews. I saw him get paid."

The men could tell from the stench that he had lain there all day. The smell would soon attract wild dogs, who might dig up the other fresh graves. They wrapped the traitor who sought notoriety for his deed in his own cloak and buried him without words or ceremony. Only his treacherous reputation survived.

Marcus and Jeshur

"Where are you going?" asked Marcus.

"To Bethlehem. We should be there by first light," answered Jeshur.

"May I go with you?" asked Marcus.

"Of course," said Jeshur. Jeshur couldn't imagine a centurion, a figure of Roman authority, asking to go home with them.

"Where do you come from?" asked Jeshur as they walked the familiar road.

"I came from the mountains near Rome. My father was a sheep herder. Our specialty was making cheese. I met Nathan and Tabitha in the market and would like to work with them."

Adah and Joanna couldn't believe their ears.

Marcus continued. "I was sent to spy on all of you. And Nathan and Tabitha are the ones who started me thinking about who Jesus is … or was. Four years ago, I joined the military in Rome to enforce peace and order established by the government. But I began to see that solving problems by force creates more problems. It takes a change of heart, a change of attitude toward others. When Nathan and Tabitha spoke kindly to me about Jesus's love, it broke my hardened heart. Now I am convinced that Jesus was God's Son. I have witnessed many crucifixions, but I've never seen such an outpouring of love and forgiveness by the one being crucified. The wonders of nature also convinced me that God is the Creator God, just as Tabitha said. I would like to learn more about him."

"Indeed you will," Jeshur agreed.

At that moment, the sound of clattering horses' hooves broke the peaceful scene. The group turned to see Crispus dismount his horse. "Halt, in the name of the Roman Empire!" he shouted. Soldiers grabbed Jeshur and Marcus. "You are under arrest!" shouted Crispus.

The women screamed and ran to Nathan, while the soldiers bound Jeshur's and Marcus' hands with cords.

"What is this? What are you doing?" shouted Marcus.

"You are under arrest for deserting the Roman Legion, Marcus. Your companion is under arrest for trying to stop a legal crucifixion," exclaimed Crispus. "We are taking you back to Jerusalem for questioning." Nathan and the women followed at a distance.

The soldiers led Jeshur and Markus to the prison beneath the Tower of Antonia. A guard opened the rusty gate and pushed them in. The gate clanged shut, confirming the reality that they were now prisoners of Rome. Insufferable night turned to ugly dawn. The other prisoners were rowdy characters being held until they were sentenced. One and all nursed the fear of their future. Jeshur shuddered in despair to think how Onam must have suffered for months, living in this dark, dank dungeon.

Nathan, Adah, and Joanna, who had retreated to Mary and Martha's house in Bethany, mercifully brought the men food and water the next morning.

"How long will you be here?" they asked anxiously.

"We will see the judge this morning," replied Jeshur. "Hopefully they will let us go when they hear our story."

Crispus brought Jeshur to a spacious office in the fortress, furnished in a way that spoke of the dignity of the Roman judge who hardly looked up from his papers. Jeshur felt beads of perspiration on his brow. Could he withstand the fear that tore at him? He braced himself.

"What is the charge?" the judge asked. His cold, sharp features emphasized his haughty Roman indifference.

"Sir, I am an eyewitness that this man tried to stop an official crucifixion of Jesus of Nazareth," explained Crispus. His brother was crucified with Jesus for robbery and insurrection.

"Is that true?" The judge glared at Jeshur.

"Yes, sir," answered Jeshur. He swallowed hard.

"What is your name?" asked the judge, giving Jeshur a passing glance.

"Jeshur, a shepherd from the house of Joel in Bethlehem, sir."

"Are you a Jew?" asked the judge, folding his hands.

"My family and I have followed the Jewish law all of our lives," Jeshur explained. He took a deep breath and felt calmer.

"Do you realize that Jesus and your own brother defied the Jewish laws?" the cynical judge probed.

"Jesus of Nazareth didn't come to break the law," replied Jeshur. "He came to give people a higher law to live by."

"And how do you know this is true?" The judge's gaze became more penetrating.

"One night when I was young, my father and brother and I were watching our sheep on a hillside near Bethlehem. An angel came from heaven, saying God had sent his Son, the Messiah, the one who would bring peace on earth. He told us where to find the baby. My brother and I actually saw him lying in a manger in a cave behind the Bethlehem Inn."

Jeshur continued, "They took Jesus and fled to Egypt to escape their enemies. Many years later I found Jesus teaching crowds of people about God's love for them. I believed him because he sounded like the very source of love. I believe he was God on earth. He performed many miracles, even brought a man back from the dead. No one could do that but God."

"So you claim to be an eyewitness of his birth? He convinced you that he was eternal God. But you also witnessed his death. How can you explain that?" the judge asked with a sneer.

"I can't explain it, sir." Jeshur grimaced and bowed his head.

The judge smirked. "If you promise to give up this foolishness, you'll receive a full pardon. If not, you will be crucified for insurrection. That will be all. Bring in the next criminal."

Jeshur reeled at the sentence and stumbled out of the room.

Crispus brought in Marcus. "Sir, this centurion has deserted the Roman army. He has disgraced the league of centurions and declared that he is now a follower of Jesus, the Nazarene who was crucified yesterday."

"Is that true?" asked the judge.

"Yes, sir," Marcus acquiesced, bowing his head.

"You gave up the Roman Legion to follow this Jewish nonsense? You know the rules. That will be death by crucifixion. However, if you change your mind by tomorrow, you can come back to the legion and there will be no questions asked. You are a good soldier, due for a promotion," added the judge.

"I will not change my mind," muttered Marcus, clenching his fists.

"Take these men back to the prison," barked the judge. He had several other miscreants to interview and seemed annoyed with the whole proceeding.

Marcus shuddered as he felt his neck hair bristle.

Back in the vermin-infested dungeon, Jeshur sat against the wall, his head in his hands, the judge's sentence ringing in his ears.

How could belief in Jesus, the Son of God, lead to my death? thought Jeshur. *What if I changed my mind? No, I could never do that. He transformed my life completely. But what will my family do with a second son in jail awaiting the death penalty?*

"Jesus never changed his story, even when he died," commented Marcus.

"That's right," Jeshur agreed. "So we must not waver."

Some of the prisoners crowded around Jeshur and asked, "What did they catch you for?"

Jeshur told them his story, knowing that they would probably laugh. It didn't matter now. The prisoners became silent and drew near. Some scoffed, but one old Samaritan cried, "I wish someone had told me about Jesus when I was young. I wouldn't be here today."

Jeshur couldn't sleep that night, the judge's sentence weighing heavily upon his mind. He remembered how shocked he was when his baby brother Ezer was murdered, how he felt when he lost his father and when Onam had died on a Roman cross. Onam's shepherd's staff hung on the wall at home next to his father's. Now his would be added.

I've lost Jesus, the Messiah I believed in with all of my heart, he reflected in despair.

He recalled that during Jesus's visit to their home, he had said, "I am the sacrificial lamb for your sins." *Did Jesus come to the world to be slain like the sacrificial lambs my father and I delivered to Jerusalem?* Now he was sentenced to be crucified along with Marcus. Another agonizing day and sleepless night passed. Jeshur dropped into a fatigued unconsciousness.

Gray dawn filtered through prison bars. Suddenly the bars and floors of the prison began to shake! Was Jeshur dreaming, or did he see the rusty gate open? An earthquake? Men rushed by him, waking him to reality. Prisoners tumbled over each other racing to freedom! Soldiers ran everywhere in panic as if lost in a maze.

Jeshur and Marcus, now free, headed toward Bethany when they met Nathan, Adah, and Joanna on their way to the dungeon to bring them food. Jeshur said, "We're free! I don't understand it, but we're free."

"Thank God!" exclaimed Adah as she hugged her firstborn. "Jeshur, Marcus, we've just seen Mary Magdalene, and she says the most incredible thing has happened. Jesus has come back from the dead."

"What?"

"Mary said she talked to him in the garden where he was buried. He is alive! He's gone to Galilee to talk to his disciples. Let's go see him too!"

Jeshur and Marcus staggered at the news. They had witnessed his death. He had been buried in a tomb only three days ago. It was hard to believe that Jesus could come back to life after all he had been through.

"A big earthquake rolled the stone away from the tomb," explained Adah.

Jeshur hugged his brother and laughed. "Our God is stronger than stones, or prison gates, or even death! We're seeing reality in process. Come, let's all go to Galilee."

The news spread quickly. Most of Jesus's disciples and others who heard the news gathered in Galilee to see if the story were true. Suddenly Jesus appeared among them. He had defeated death. They bowed and worshiped him in utter amazement. He acknowledged their praise and raised his hand to speak. People gasped and then moaned as they looked at his fresh nail prints.

"Peace be with you," he began. "Because you have seen me, you have believed. Blessed are those who have not seen and yet will believe. I am going to my Father, but one day I shall return."

As Jesus mingled with the small group, giving encouragement and assurance, his eyes fell on Adah and Joanna, who were talking to his mother. He took their hands as they knelt before him, in great awe.

"Adah, Joanna, thank you for your loyalty. You have proven your steadfast love for me. You are my sisters. Continue to spread my love to others. Many will believe in me because of your witness."

"Yes, Master."

He gazed at Jeshur and Nathan with such love in his eyes—more than the shepherds had ever felt before, more than they even thought possible. Jesus stretched out his scarred hands. The shepherds knelt and clasped the hands of their Savior.

"I will always be with you, Jeshur and Nathan. You are my friends and eyewitnesses of my love for the world. How will people know of my love unless you tell them?"

Is he talking to us? wondered Jeshur. His heart beat wildly. He was overwhelmed with many excuses for not being worthy of such a request. In a timeless moment, his life flashed before him. He was just a poor shepherd, not good with words. His brother had been crucified alongside of Jesus. He was an escaped convict, doomed to death, hair streaked with gray, a family and sheep to care for. The brothers glanced at each other and then at Jesus. Suddenly, they heard once again the music of the angels.

"Yes, my Lord."

> When they had seen him, they spread the word concerning what had been told them about Jesus, and all who heard it were amazed at what the shepherds said to them. The shepherds returned, glorifying and praising God for all the things they had heard and seen, which were just as they had been told. (Luke 2:17, 20 NIV)

Epilogue

"Mother, guess what? I'm going to be a shepherd in the Christmas pageant at church!" said Noel. "My Sunday school teacher chose Joe and me. We get to walk down the aisle and stand by the baby Jesus in the manger while the choir sings 'Silent Night.'"

"How wonderful," responded his mother. "I think it is very appropriate since our name is 'Shepherd.' We'll have to get to work on your costume and find a shepherd's staff."

"Mom, do you think that's why I'm playing the part of a shepherd? Do you think our ancestors really were shepherds that saw baby Jesus?" asked Noel.

"Shepherds raise sheep in many parts of the world," his mother answered. "Then there are those God calls to be like shepherds to guide people to the truth of his word. Our pastor is like a shepherd because he preaches and teaches the Bible. He also does many other things to help people. But we also can become shepherds by telling people that long ago Jesus came to the world to tell people how God loves them and calls them to follow him."

"Here's my line," said Noel. "The angel said, 'Glory to God in the highest. And on earth, peace and good will to all people.' What does 'good will' mean?"

"Good will is giving gifts or helping others in some way," his mother explained. "Many people don't realize why the Christmas season brings such happiness. All around the world children get excited, go to parties, go caroling. People sing beautiful music explaining the Christmas story.

People think of others instead of themselves when they shop for gifts and plan celebrations. Merchants are happy because people spend more money at Christmas. More people find jobs. Employees get extra pay. People give to charity. This all happens because of Jesus's birth."

Noel hurried to his room to learn his lines for the Christmas pageant, humming as he ran.

Acknowledgments

I am deeply indebted to the many people who helped and inspired me in the writing of this novel. I thank experts in the field, Dr. Jerome Browne, Dr. Tony Cartledge, and Louise Caldwell, for their time spent reading and giving input to the story in its various stages. I thank my children, David Hill and Jana Gillham, who are both talented writers for their help and encouragement. I thank my church historian husband, Les, for his wisdom and contribution concerning certain historical matters and for taking me to Israel for a wonderful on-sight experience. My illustrator and friend, Rae House, gave much helpful advice. I am deeply grateful to my editor, Ann Tonks, an experienced writer, who was a tremendous help.

About the Author

Jan Hill grew up in Oklahoma, attended Southwestern Baptist Theological Seminary, and served as a Southern Baptist missionary in Southeast Asia for thirty-eight years with her husband, Dr. D. Leslie Hill. They lived in the Philippines, Thailand, and Singapore, ministering to missionaries and aiding in their work in six countries in Southeast Asia, where Dr. Hill worked as an administrator. In the Philippines, Jan taught her three children, directed choirs, led in the planting of a new church, taught English and music, and led women's Bible studies. She served as the reporter for the Philippine Baptist Mission for many years and wrote numerous articles for various Baptist publications in the United States. She published a short story on Mary, the Mother of Jesus, in a popular Filipino women's magazine. She has authored a children's missionary study, *Friends of India*, published by the International Mission Board, *A Cook's Tour, Favorite Recipes of Missionary Homemakers, Beautiful Feet of Women in Missions*, and compiled stories covering the first fifty years of the Philippine Baptist Mission called *Let the Philippine Islands Be Glad*. This is her first novel. Jan is also a singer and a harpist. She has recorded two albums, *Christmas Harp Carols* and *A Harpist's Garden, Songs and Hymns*. In retirement, the Hills have made several trips back to the Philippines to teach at the Philippine Baptist Seminary. Jan is a music therapist at Baptist Health in Lexington, Kentucky.

Printed in the United States
By Bookmasters